The Journal of Bran Ayton

Published by: Menhir Books

Cover Design: www.birdandcroft.com

Contact us: hello@branayton.com

More about Bran: www.branayton.com

ISBN: 978-1-5272-5383-4

Menhir
Books

This Book & How it Works

About The Journal of Bran Ayton

In the Journal of Bran Ayton we read Bran's personal reflections in the first person over forty days. Within a strong narrative, Bran reflects on his life and relationships, wanders through a range of digressions and reveals his own idiosyncrasies, just as you or I would in any journal we might keep. Don't be surprised to find Bran drawing on information and characters appearing from nowhere! After all this is his journal, giving a glimpse into Bran's private world without the gloss of having to please anyone.

On each day of his journal, Bran reflects on some aspect his life. Beginning in a somewhat faltering way he asks questions of himself and his understanding of life and death. Some of what he writes is quite serious, in its way. That said, there's nothing any one of us wouldn't consider at some point. Throughout his journal, Bran finds his voice and explores experiences, topics and relationships important to him.

One of the themes running through the journal is Bran's relationship with Pearl, his former girlfriend from years ago. She reappeared in Bran's life roughly a year before he began to keep this journal. Describing herself as 'dressing like a hooker,' Pearl has a reputation for being alcohol dependent and chaotic. Bran on the other hand has reputation for being ordered, measured and successful.

Characters drift in and out of Bran's journal. For example Eli the barmaid and her belief in vegan werewolves, Boatman Bob with his accidental wisdom, Peado Ronnie, Aunty Doris & Aunty Mary, Frank & Maria the Italian-American cafe owners and of course Tess. We can't forget Donna and Carolyn, important in their own way. There are others too, people who build texture into Bran's life. That's how life is. People create texture.

How to Read The Journal of Bran Ayton

Hopefully readers will find there is a strong narrative running through Bran's journal, such that someone could read from Day 1 to Day 40, as if they were reading any other novel. However the book has been written with the expectation that some will want to read a section (or a day) at a time. In which case, it should take between 15 and 30 minutes for the average reader to read each section quite slowly. There will be some who prefer to dip in and out of Bran's journal. That's fine. A bit of the narrative will be missed either side of the section/day that is read. It's OK to dip in here and there. To some extent each section is complete in itself. So if a section/day seems not so appealing to jump across it to the next one. The reader can always go back and fill any gaps. Really. It's fine.

The Journal of Bran Ayton and Real Life

None of the characters in the book are real. Everyone is imagined. Therefore, any resemblance to people living or dead is purely coincidental.

Although a work of fiction, Bran's journal pokes into reality. In fact some places in the book are influenced by real life. For example, we learn that Bran's motivation for writing his journal comes from discovering his ninth great grandfather's memoir. This echoes of my own experience. I 'discovered' my own ninth great grandfather's memoir. His real name was Jonathan Priestley and he wrote, 'Memoirs of the Priestley Family'. I've included a link to the memoir in the footnotes.[1]

Written at the end of a long life in 1696 and after a period of monumental turmoil in England, Jonathan wrote these words that have become important for me:

> *"What a Labyrinth of sorrow is the life of man; of good men as well as of others, for all things come alike to all; but not withstanding, there is a vast difference"*[2]

Although not recorded in his memoir, Jonathan Priestley had a son named Nathaniel who knew the famous diarist and author of Robinson Crusoe, Daniel Defoe.

Robinson Crusoe was a work of fiction, written in the first person as a journal. Some readers mistakenly thought it an actual, firsthand account of the real Crusoe's adventures. Similarly, The Journal of Bran Ayton is a work of fiction written in the first person. In that sense, it is just not true.

In Defoe's story, York was Robinson Crusoe's home town and he sailed off on his adventures from Hull in Yorkshire. It won't take long for any reader to spot both direct and indirect references to York and Hull in the Journal of Bran Ayton, along with other places around Yorkshire such as Beverley, Pontefract, Wakefield and elsewhere. As a matter of fact, Hull was the inspiration for the town of Elsternwick in Bran's journal, while Saxby was inspired by York.

Incidentally, the Buttercross referred to in Bran's journal is based on one in Pontefract marketplace, outside St Giles' church. Perhaps the reader might like to try and identify different places in Bran's journal whether around Yorkshire or in Amsterdam, Florence, Bordeaux, New York or even Lancashire.

Michael Croft
December 2019

---

[1] https://archive.org/details/memoirsofpriestl00durh/page/n8

[2] The Memoir of Jonathan Priestley, 1696 - https://archive.org/details/memoirsofpriestl00durh/page/n7

Acknowledgement

I am indebted to Dr Stephen Gibbs PhD for his friendship, encouragement and critical support as 'literary editor' of The Journal of Bran Ayton.

'No man is an island, entire of itself; every man is a piece of the continent, a part of the main'

John Donne (1572-1631)

A Beginning

He doesn't seem to be paying attention.

I think it's probably his mother sitting across the table from him.

I love the muted colours in the scene. A shaft of sunlight from the ceiling is lighting the young man's face.

It's like a van Gogh, the ones about ordinary people.

The last time I was in Amsterdam I spent hours at the Rijks Museum looking at scenes such as this.

The one seems somehow tragic.

Of course I'm reading into it.

I can't know it's tragic.

It's just what I feel looking in.

I wish the scene was hanging on my wall at home.

The one I take to be the young man's mother has served my coffee for years.

I don't know the young man, although I've watched him grow.

I don't know the mother, either. I don't even know her name.

The little tableau was soon gone.

I turned and looked out of the cafe window into Minster Square as the young man walked over to the table next to mine. He's whey-face and pale. Somehow sad.

He came over to join a friend. He's the busker who plays under the arch of the Buttercross. I've stopped to listen before now.

I'm never sure about buskers.

I don't know where the divide is between the beggar and the troubadour?

It's wrong but I'm straining to listen to their conversation. I keep catching phrases about this and that.

Evidently they have strong opinions.

Young men are like that.

The busker is fine-boned with short-cropped, mousy hair, a waxed moustache, bright blue eyes and tattoos.

I've come to like tattoos. I imagine most people would be surprised. I don't mean I like Popeye, anchor tattoos, or the kind people who spit in the street have. I mean tattoos that say something, are individual and up-close and personal.

I can't hear what they're saying, but sense what's being talked about.

I'm picking up crumbs, like a beggar while I drink my coffee and eat my almond croissant.

I'd love to join in.

I feel I need to distract myself so look out of the cafe window.

The market in Minster Square is a bustling with people as usual. It's been like this for centuries. I don't know what's changed.

I can see the cheese stall. The stout, red-faced woman with frizzy hair is serving customers and slipping a sliver of cheese in her mouth between each one.

I like that word, 'stout'. It feels a forbidden these days. I don't know why. I buy from her every week. She greets me with my name. 'Morning Bran,' she says.

I've no idea how she knows my name.

It's been in my family for generations. Sometimes I feel it possesses me rather than me it. There's one in every generation, a Bran. In fact I'm just connecting my name to the DNA test I've just done. It turns out I'm 37% Celtic Yorkshire. Apparently I'm of this place, as much as anyone can be.

People assume my name's an abbreviation, but it's just Bran. It means 'raven'. I've always thought it odd, but it's my name. There's not much I can do about it.

I'm enjoying writing in this notebook.

It's the first time I've tried to write anything.

I bought it at Pickering's. They've been there as long as I can remember.

8

Mrs Pickering still serves on.

I don't know how they keep going.

I'd not been in for years.

When I paid for my notebook, Mrs Pickering put it in a pink candy-striped bag and said 'Good day Mr Ayton'. We passed a word or two. She said I reminded her of dad.

They used pink, candy-stripped bags when I was a child.

It doesn't smell. The bag I mean. I think it should. They used them for the penny mix in Aunty Doris and Peado Ronnie's shop when I was a child. I was allowed one every Friday, a penny mix I mean.

I bought a new fountain pen at Pickering's as well.

It felt right. I don't know why.

The card from Scarab is on the table next to my satchel. I'm going to use it as a bookmark.

I'll call this notebook, my 'journal' and begin by writing about ordinary things that come to mind. I suppose the young men at the next table and the woman on the cheese stall are beginnings.

I fancy myself as a bit of an Alan Bennett.

I met him once. I was with mum. We were at a crossing in Boar Lane, near Leeds station. I wasn't paying attention. Mum stepped out. We hadn't noticed the lights on the crossing change to green. He made some quip as I caught mum's arm and helped her back onto the pavement, then he was gone.

I like to think of it as meeting Alan Bennett. It wasn't that. We were just in the same place, at the crossing.

I digress.

There's a book on the table where the two young men are sitting. I can see it's, The Remains of Elmet[3]. I have a copy. Ted Hughes was a bit too dark for me until I read

---

[3] T. Hughes, The Remains of Elmet, Harper Collins (1979)

9

that book. It helped me dig behind his layers. I like to think I began to see where he was coming from.

I'm surprised to see it.

I've no business being surprised. It's just that I am.

Why shouldn't one or other of the young men read Ted Hughes?

Seeing them with the book has sparked a memory of a line in the poem, Rhododendron:
> *"Ugly as a brass band in India"*[4]

I hate rhododendrons.

I dug them out of my garden.

I don't think they belong.

I can't help being drawn back to the snatches of conversation from the next table. I'm straining to hear. I don't know what they're talking about. It's more in their manner I can tell they feel strongly.

Someone once told me 'passion and naivety are gifts of the young'. I don't know if they were quoting someone. It sounded like a saying.

I read about two young men the other day in Jonathan Ayton, my ninth great grandfather's memoir. One was his son Nathaniel, the other Daniel Defoe. It seems they were friends and Daniel was inciting Nathaniel to rebel against the king.

It turns out Jonathan had rebelled when he was young. He writes about being involved in what he calls Booth's Uprising and he was a Presbyterian Royalist. I'd not heard of either the uprising or Presbyterian Royalists. It seems the rebellion came to nothing and Jonathan just about got away with his life.

I'm trying to imagine what it would take for the two at the next table to have their strong views spill into rebellion?

I wonder what it would feel like to rebel and go on some crusade or other?

I want to feel it, but can't.

---

[4] T. Hughes, The Remains of Elmet, Harper Colins (1979)

Dad was in the war. I never knew what he did. He never said.

He was fanatical war shouldn't happen again.

I remember the Falklands war.

We worried we'd get called up.

It was on TV. They say it was the first televised war. Soldiers and real blood, in our drawing room after tea. We're numb to it now. That kind of thing is on TV all the time.

When I was at school, we learned about the times Jonathan Ayton lived through. Elsternwick was overrun by Robert Lilburne and his army in 1647. I remember the date. Jonathan would have only been a boy.

When I was at school, we remembered Lilburne's siege of Elsternwick in playground games and the projects we did. I seem to remember he was a Leveller, a Puritan fighting a holy war. We learned he tore, Elsternwick apart. I suppose they'd call it Jihad these days.

What was that playground game and the rhyme we sang. It was a bit like Tigg?

I think it went something like this:
1.2.3.4.5, run and hide, run and hide
Lilburne's coming, Lilburne's coming!
1,2,3,4,5, run and hide, run and hide,
He'll blow your tower down.

We all stood at one end of the playground, except the person who was 'Lilburne'. They stood in the middle. They closed their eyes and said those lines:
1.2.3.4.5, run and hide, run and hide
Lilburne's coming, Lilburne's coming!
We had to run to the other end and touch the wall as 'Lilburne' tried to catch us.

It was only a playground game.

It was no game for Jonathan.

He had to run and hide when Lilburne came.

In his memoir, Jonathan wrote about hiding in 'the Tower' and running from there to the castle as he tried to escape. It must have been terrifying.

The siege of the castle lasted all winter. Canons blew buildings apart. They brought miners to dig under the Curtain Wall at the top of Sally Lane. The wall fell down and the castle was overrun.

I can't imagine the terror.

The two at the next table are getting up to go. I wonder if they listened to stories growing up. They can't have dropped into this world from nowhere. At least one of them has Ted Hughes' poems, or at least he has a book of them.

Words are drifting from the back of my mind to the front. I know them well enough:
> *Nothing in the world is single;*
> *All things by a law divine*
> *In one spirit meet and mingle.*
> *Why not I with thine?*[5]

I can't say why those words came to mind. Perhaps it's seeing the young men hug as the busker left, Ted Hughes in hand.

There's something in me envies that hug. It's struck a chord for me somehow.

I'm digressing.

I don't know whether journals should stick to the point or wander round whatever comes into the mind.

I'm going to have to find out.

The last dregs of my coffee have gone cold. I want to write about one more thing before I leave. It's come to mind because of the words from that poem I jotted down. It's that phrase '*meet and mingle*'. I don't think for a minute, what I'm about to write is even close to what was in the mind of the person who first penned those words. (I think it was Shelley?)

I don't know what it means when people say they have a 'connection' but I know what it feels like to have one. I can't put it into words. I suppose I'm getting a sense that I need to search for the *meet and mingle* of connections.

For example, there's that story of Christopher Fleet I grew up with. I suppose it's more legend or folklore than anything but I connect with him somehow. Maybe it's just that a bit of me wants to be a hero like him. I think we all do deep down.

---

[5] Shelley, Percy Bysshe. *The Selected Poetry and Prose of Shelley.* Ware, Hertfordshire, UK: The Wordsworth Poetry Library (2002).

I remember the story about Christopher Fleet was keeping watch in the Toll House at Pullen Bridge when the vanguard of Lilburne's army marched up the coast road, he lured them into the sands along the foreshore until they were 'swallowed' then followed 'Secret Ways' to the beacon on the Look Out so Elsternwick could be warned and the earl spirited away.

I don't know how true it is.

I don't suppose it matters.

Jonathan wrote something I've committed to memory.

> *"What a Labyrinth of Sorrow is the life of man; of good men as well as of others, for all things come alike to all; but not withstanding, there is a vast difference"*[6]

I like it, but it makes me wonder what a good man is?

I'm not sure about this business of writing a journal. I sense I'll need to find my own 'secret way', whatever that is.

---

[6] The Memoir of Jonathan Priestley, 1696 - https://archive.org/details/memoirsofpriestl00durh/page/n7

Bran's Journal

Day 1

I'm hesitant about writing the first proper entry in my journal.

I'm going to begin by testing the waters.

I'll start by thinking about a simple thing, like coming home at the end of the day.

Actually, I love that feeling when the front door closes and the world outside loses its significance. For a few hours outside becomes no more than a footprint in wet sand. Within my threshold everything feels more solid and certain.

Today when I shut the door and looked in the hall mirror my eyes wandered across my reflection to the painting on the wall behind me. I've always loved it. It's an impression of a river in sweeps of blues and greys and whites with a meadow beyond peppered by flowers of yellow and orange. The meadow's backdrop is the edge of a dark forest. It looks a beautiful place, although I wonder about that forest. You have to look carefully; there's a young girl painted into the picture. You can see her in the brushstrokes, on the other side of the river. She's why I bought the painting.

The place where I'm writing is my most private space, tucked away above my bedroom. I call it the Cupola room.

I was inspired to build it after visiting the Cathedral of Santa Maria del Fiore in Florence. I felt very small there. I liked that. It felt like my whole life was summed up under the cathedral's cupola dome. I wanted my own. It's a place I can be small and unnoticed.

I project the night sky on the inside of my cupola dome and watch the constellations pivot around the Pole Star. I'm content and at peace as I watch. In my smallness I'm at the centre of this spinning cosmos.

Floor to ceiling windows support the cupola. I can see for miles. I can see the Sax estuary widen to the sea far off in the east. On a clear day, I can see the road on the north bank, from the ruined Bastille at Pullen Bridge and east along the road to Elsternwick. I can just make out the Look Out. I know each rise and fall of that road.

I met someone once who said, 'you're either from Elsternwick or you're not'. I've tried to say I'm from somewhere else. Sometimes, I've tried to be from no-where. Deep down I know where I'm from.

That's enough for day one.

I need to lie back and take in those stars; my universe.

Day 2

The view from the Cupola room is incredible. I can see the Sax estuary glistening a grey shimmer where the sky meets the water.

The view sends me to another place.

That said, Kevin Linn has broken into my thoughts, Tom's older brother.

It's frustrating.

I would've preferred to stay in that other place, taking in the view but Kevin and the line of the far distant horizon are competing from my attention.

He reappeared in my life last year and hasn't quite left.

His arrival was typically sudden and unexpected.

He'd do that when we were young, suddenly be there.

It turns out he has lung cancer and it's terminal.

I'm struggling with it, if I'm honest.

I don't know why, but I want to cry.

I don't cry easily.

I picture Kevin out there on the grey, glistening shimmer of the estuary. Perhaps that's why I thought of him: cold and drifting on cold water.

I wonder if I'm somehow grieving for him.

I'm not sure.

It's difficult to be sure.

Every year, the church says, *'Media vita in morte sumus'* 'in the midst of life we are in death'.

Kevin is dying.

There's something good about him.

There's something good about Tom too. Mum used to say, 'He's just a good natured lad'.

Kevin told me Tom's been caught up in what he called a 'web of deceit'. He said some woman called 'the Bitch' had tangled him in a mess. It was dreadful to hear, more dreadful than hearing about Kevin's cancer in a way.

I asked who this 'bitch' was. He said she's known in the family as 'she who shall not be named'. Evidently, their father, wanted wipe her from their minds in order to move on.

I gave Kevin my contact details and he gave me Tom's. We haven't been in touch. I suppose too much time has passed.

I want to write about something I learned from Kevin that's come to mind.

I'm struck by his interest in how I was, even in light of his illness and Tom's troubles

It was difficult hearing Kevin. He could only whisper.

He asked, 'How's Margaret?'

I wonder what he remembered?

He was always Tom's big brother, bad influence and a little wild. Six years older than us he'd been away and come back. He ran away to the trawlers and then the rigs.

He was always winsome and knowing.

Lucky bastard!

He'd always something interesting to say, oozing risk.

I've always stumbled with introductions.

I was the quiet lad in the corner.

I bet he's a better friend than me.

I'm a bastard!

I didn't know about Tom.

What kind of friend am I?

I wonder who this nameless bitch might be?

I'm trying to get back to my point about Kevin, with his frail-faint voice.

It's interesting how I get distracted with my rambling thoughts.

I've heard it said, something's not real unless it's experienced. I don't suppose a person who dies can know the experience of death. I understand death is a threshold to somewhere else, except for those grieving?

It's a paradox.

Kevin will die. I will too. If death isn't real for the person dying, except as this threshold, does anyone really die?

I suppose at its at the heart of what we believe: we travel from this world to somewhere better. We carry on. I guess we want to call that heaven. I see that.

There's a kind of hell in the thought of not existing, of being wiped out, no-one remembering our name.

What a thought to be condemned: no-one remembering.

Kevin used to sit with us in the Snug at the Queens. We'd listen to his stories.

It's strange how I bumped into him at the Queens last year.

The Queens is all mock Edwardian now, with smart menus and designer lagers. I think the designers tried too hard. I remember one item on the menu that made me laugh:
> *'Pan-fried Langoustine with cripple-cooked fries and lemon-glazed Samphire.'*

It was Scampi and Chips in my day.

I remember reading that typing error and chuckling.

It's not a word that's allowed these days: cripple.

Kevin's confidence has been replaced with breathless anxiety.

I had to listen carefully.

He spoke of someone called Jan, calling her his 'Soulmate' and the 'Love of His Life'. In his faded voice, he spoke of life with her, the times they'd shared. He began to weep, his hand quivering and reaching for mine as he told me they'd parted.

21

I was struck by a vast silence, an augmented breath punctuating what he had to say,

I tried to recall times with Tom and spoke of 'Tom and I.'

He scolded me. 'It's not, Tom and I. It's Tom and me'.

I had nowhere to go.

It felt so trivial.

He corrected my grammar.

We hugged as I left him. He'd never done that before. It was the hug of a brother.

It's wrong but the question of grammar consumed me. I still feel embarrassed by it.

He was right. I should've said, 'Tom and me' not 'Tom and I'.

I know the rules.

'Me' the subjective pronoun, describing my window on the world, the person looking out.

'I' the objective pronoun, the 'who' (or the 'whom') others see.

It's 'me' in my Cupola room, looking at the stars projected on the ceiling.

There's the question: 'what about, me?'

'I' can present to life and the world as confident, competent, professional successful.

'Me' quakes.
      Is uncertain.
            Is suspicious.
Is hopeful.
      Is vain.
            Is.......whatever.
'Tom and me'.
      'Tom and I'.

It's not about grammar.

It's about knowing Tom, not just his name.

Day 3

I thought a lot about Uncle Trevor today. I've no idea why.

He had a gift for stories.

They came thick and fast.

He told them with sparkling, pin-sharp, blue eyes set in a broad grin that came with an infectious, machine-gun laugh.

Once he took me to one side and said, 'Bran, when you meet someone new, always tell them a little story about something that happened in the past week'. I've never forgotten his advice, although I've never been very good at story-telling.

I'm not sure his stories were true. I still laughed when he told them. I don't suppose mattered whether or not they were true; I mean literally truth. They were like a clever card trick, sleight of hand drawing you in.

Stories tumble out of everyone, lubricating relationships.

I like those phrases, 'stories tumble out' and 'lubricating relationships'. I didn't plan them.

The other evening in the pub I surprised myself by telling Steve my story about Pearl.

He knew we met again last year. I'd not told him we text and talk every day.

He think's I'm infatuated. He thinks I'm looking for frisson and impropriety.

I did protest.

He pressed, 'he protests too much!'

Isn't it funny how phrases like 'he protests too much' pop out.

Steve's wrong!

I spoke the truth.

There's no frisson.

It is weird though.

I trespassed on something special, mentioning Pearl.

I like to keep relationships apart.

Blurred lines divide friendships.

Stories cross thresholds between people.

I can't keep Pearl completely separate and preserved for me, much as I would love to.

The conversation with Steve made me think about why I call her Pearl.

It's not her name.

She's Margaret really, Margaret Fleet.

I've always called her Pearl.

I like it.

We spoke today.

She told me she's due to visit Selwyn and suggested we meet for coffee before she catches her train to Cambridge.

I hardly see her, so that will be nice.

'Nice' God I hate that word. It's bland pleasantry.

I call Pearl my 'happy place'. I don't know why. I suppose deep down, she knows me and I know her.

She's woven into my life.

I like the image of being woven in.

People weave in amongst, crossing and re-crossing between one another, working together.

I'm taking a moment to look out of the windows.

From up here in my Cupola room, I can see river barges ploughing up and down the estuary. They remind me of Ben.

When I was a boy, I'd sit on the harbour wall watching Ben getting his barge ready for the next trip. He was a bargee, one of the men who worked the great, broad river barges. He was a lumbering man with huge, gnarled hands and a bulbous red nose that dribbled constantly from the centre of his weathered face. He had enquiring, deep-set eyes that had retreated from the river's winds and never quite come back to the surface. They ignited with warmth whenever he spoke of the river.

I loved Ben's stories.

He lived for the river with its currents and sandbanks, its flow and its ebb.

I wish I could be like that.

I've always focused on what might be, not what is.

I suppose Ben went with the flow, because he knew the flow.

There's that saying, 'go with the flow'. I've always thought it meant just drifting, without a sense of purpose. It might mean that. Then again Ben went with the flow but didn't drift aimlessly. He knew the flow to go with.

There feels something important in this.

I want to take a few moments to look out across the estuary.

I love this view.

I can see the north bank and the coast road cutting through treacherous sands. It's a barren place cutting Elsternwick off.

Day 4

I've dug out my memory box. It was at the back of my closet. I haven't looked in it in years.

Aunty Mary gave it to me.

I can picture her.

She wore a nylon overall that always seemed decorated by dribbled, dried egg yoke. Her false teeth clicked as she spoke.

It's funny how things come to mind.

There was always tea in the pot. I can almost taste it, steaming, stewed and in an old stained mug that was only ever rinsed. I can feel it heavy in my hand.

She'd to say things like, 'You're a go-getter, Bran.' I never knew what she meant.

It's funny how tiny memories bubble to the surface.

I'm no expert but I think the box is made of walnut. The hinge is broken. It's always been like that.

I would be about eight when she gave it to me.

Her shop was along Sally Lane, just over the bridge at Warden's Gylle. I cycled there. I remember the wet leaves on the ground and the rain pouring down. Closing my eyes for a moment, I can feel the cold water spraying up and soaking my trousers as I cycled through puddles and sodden autumn leaves. I can feel my flushed red-raw cheeks and icy-cold fingers.

The sneck on the shop door was stiff. You had to force it down and push hard to open the door. At least I did as an eight year old. The doorbell jangled.

I'm trusting my memory. I can't say with certainty what I'm writing is accurate. That matters less than allowing memories onto the page.

I remember Aunty Mary pushing through the raggedy strips of the old plastic fly screen separating the shop from her parlour. She spent her days studying the racing form back there, her black and white TV constantly playing.

She was tiny, bent double with arthritis; hands gnarled, twisted and covered in newsprint from the papers she used to wrap up the veg.

She wore marquisate rings and a broach of blue and red stones shaped like a butterfly. I reckon they must have been topaz and garnet. Old hands and a nylon overall don't go with costume jewellery. Even when I was a boy I knew that.

She'd tell me stories.

I would question and question and question.

On the day she gave me my box, it was on the table in her parlour. She told me box had always been in the family.

She said it was a place to keep memories and find the answers to all the questions in my head.

I never keep things, at least I haven't for years.

I've never been good at looking back.

I've never really gone back on principle. I don't know why I wrote,'on principle'. It's not a principle. It's a practice, a habit. I just don't do it.

Looking back is like looking at myself in the mirror. I might not like what I see in that lonely mirror.

I can feel her arms around my shoulders and her saying, 'Bran, never forget'.

I know I forgot. I got caught up with life, wondering what might be next in life.

I suppose Aunty Mary was saying, 'Pause. Take a breath. Take time to look around.'

I didn't.

I think I've lost my bearings.

I can admit to it here where no-one will see; to lose your bearings is frightening.

If I'm honest, sometimes I just don't know which way to turn.

I think I'll keep the Memory box by my chair up here in the Cupola room, so I can rummage through every now and then.

Day 5

I've been rummaging through old coins and stamps, photographs and press-cuttings in my Memory Box. I found dad's medals from the Second World War and granddad's from the First. My swimming medals amongst them. I couldn't make sense of a strange old key with a cloth tag tied to it. I remember, it was in there when Aunty Mary gave me the box, along with a bit of old hinge.

I came across a press-cutting near the bottom of the box. It's been torn from the Elsternwick Courier. There isn't a date. I am guessing it would've been the mid '70s. The photograph in the cutting has been taken at the ruins of the Temple on the Stryd above Elsternwick. It's of a whole crowd of us with Father Francis.

I wonder what everyone's doing now?

Tom and Austin are with me in the photograph.

Pearl is dangling her legs off the end of the Temple's plinth. Her back is against a column. Jem is with her. She oozed confidence in her quiet, quirky way. Pearl always seemed so disengaged.

I can see Debbie and Martin and Neville and Donna. Neville was so small. He used to try and make himself taller, standing on his tiptoes. Donna was a proper 'fat lass'.

There's Simon with Mark and David.

I struggled with David. I found him a bit frightening.

I can see Janet at the back with her frizzy hair.

I can't wind the clock back, but wonder how things might've been if I'd done that one thing differently.

Mark did well at school. I heard he gave up and threw himself off the Gorge Bridge.

Simon, threw his chances away, sent down for pissing on the Quad. I've seen him at a distance. He looked a wreck. His parents pinned so many hopes on him.

I wander about the faces in the photograph but keep going back to Austin. I find thinking about him difficult; the first person I knew who died.

So young!

Tragic.

I tried to pushed the experience away, to bury it. To bury Austin.

It was too soon.

He was too young.

Then again Simon.

I wonder what hell he went through?

I don't suppose he's the sort of person I'd have round to dinner. I don't suppose he'd want to drink Pimms on my terrace.

From what Pearl tells me, I'm just redundant conventionality compared to him.

Actually whilst the description fell off the end of my pen, it sums me up pretty well.

Is conventionality so bad? It is 'me'. I just don't like the idea of being redundant.

What about Tom? We were more brothers than friends.

I wronged him.

It was a long time ago.

I was too proud, too stubborn.

A small thing became large.

It started out no bigger than a speck of grit in a shoe.

When you get grit it your shoe it can feel like a boulder.

So much to think about.

Day 6

I went for coffee with Pearl this morning. It was a bit early for me. Never mind. I enjoyed the walk to the cafe at the station.

I can't work out why I feel so comfortable with her. I suppose it's what they call a 'connection', whatever one of those is.

There was a flip in my stomach at the thought of meeting her. Why wouldn't there be? I hadn't seen her for months.

We were together for just half an hour as she waited for her connection to Cambridge.

It was just a few snatched minutes.

I sometimes wonder if she wants to actually meet me, rather than talk or text. We're in touch single day without fail. I think she avoids meeting face-to-face. I've no idea why.

She's bewilders me.

Each week I tot up the time we speak on the phone - typically around two hours and forty minutes. - It's been like that for a year. We've met maybe three or four times, always for a quick coffee, never more.

I've tried to talk to her about this 'connection';,' this feeling comfortable. She passes over it, telling me I 'over-think'. I know It's 'not normal' as mum used to say. Then again, I'm not sure normal matters.

Anyway, I arrived at the station cafe in good time. It was crowded with commuters. I bought the coffees. Americano for me, Skinny Latte for her. I can never resist those caramel wafers.

I sat at the back of the cafe and saw her come in.

My stomach flipped (again).

I've not seen her look like that. Her hair was pulled back in a tight pony tail of ash blond. She wore a black leather biker jacket that'd never seen a bike and black jeans that told the world she'd not lost her figure.

There was leopard print. Each time I've seen her there's been leopard print. Today, it was Chelsea boots and a chiffon scarf.

I got up to greet her and made an arse of myself. I tried to reach across a chair to hug her. She did that thing she does. She tucks her head away and down. There's no chance of even a mock-kiss never mind a real one, except in a paternal or accidentally gesture to her hair.

I can never get the hang of mock-kisses. I don't know whether to kiss once, twice or three times on the cheek, or even whether to just do a feigned kiss to one side, always avoiding any contact between lips and face. Give me a handshake any day.

Just how is it, there's a stomach flip and at the same time such awkwardness greeting someone I barely see but have known my whole life?

It's weird.

I could be misreading the situation. That said, I don't know what 'situation' I'm misreading. I just go with it.

I'm probably just being an arse.

She put her scarf on the table beside the book she'd been carrying. It was well-thumbed. I couldn't see the full title but was intrigued by the word Manifesta in the title.[7] I like the word's sound when I say it out loud. We don't use it. We say manifesto. Manifesta is the feminine form.

Manifesto, manifesta: masculine, feminine; is there much of a difference?

She's the one who talks about our 'connection'. She won't say what she means. If I ever ask, she tells me I 'over think' and that she'll get cross if go on about it, so I settle into 'the moment' as people seem to say these days.

The thing is, I feel at ease with her, in my 'moment'.

Something about her terrifies me. I don't know why.

I feel vulnerable and comfortable at the same time.

If anyone was to ask me, I'd not be able to frame my thoughts.

There's more than being in the moment about being with her. There's something prescient about our relationship, if 'relationship' is what it is.

Prescient is a better word than present.

---

[7] Manifesta, Young Women, Feminism & the Future, J Baumgardener & A Richards, Farrar, Strauss & Giroux (2000)

Being with her is about what's right, what's hopeful deep down for me. I can't frame it in words. It's odd.

There's that line about the inadequacy of words:
'Words are there for those with promises to keep'.[8]

Yes, I think it's better framed without words, just accepting. With Pearl promises would frighten me and I'm sure she'd run a mile.

I can't pin it all down.

I'm glad I can't.

I don't want hope to bubble to the surface and spoil in some aspiration or expectation that will burst. Maybe she doesn't either. Perhaps that's why we hug as we do.

We chatted so long over coffee she nearly missed her train and got up with a rush, forgetting her scarf. I brought it home with me. It's hanging in the hall.

Annoyingly, hanging up the scarf reminded me of the envelope she gave me ages ago. I'd left it in the pocket of my brown leather jacket.

I bought it maybe 25 years ago and wear it every winter. I thought it made me look like the 'Marlborough Man' in the old adverts. We've been through a lot together. I'd like to say, I'd forgotten about the envelope. In fact I'd stuffed it in the jacket pocket secretly wanting to forget about it.

The letter's front of me now. It's difficult reading. It says this:

> *Bran*
>
> *It seems like yesterday you left. You knew what life was for me and still you left. I ought to think, 'Bran, you bastard!' More than anyone, you know how people see me. That's not who I am. You know that.*
>
> *You compounded my chaos. You did that, Bran. I need you to know, that's how I see it.*
>
> *Clean, ordered, self-contained, successful Bran. You thought what you did was OK. You bastard.*

---

[8] W.H.Auden, Selected Poems. Faber & Faber (2002)

You of all people know I'm not who I appear to be.

You, you are blind to yourself.

You think you're one thing but you're another. You think you're in control but you're out of control. You live a fairyland reality. You're a lie, a deception.

Who is in chaos? Not me. You. When will you wake up!

When we were young, you were the one person, the one hope I had.

You left me.

Now you show up as if the world owes you.

I found it disturbing meeting you again, with no warning. For days afterwards, I couldn't escape thoughts of you.

I don't know what business you had appearing after all these years, but you're here now. So, against my better judgement I'm going with the flow of this.

Just don't run out on me again, you selfish bastard! – I have to get it out and say it. I won't say it again.

Call me sometime. – Just do it.

Margaret

She's right, I did walk away all those years ago. We were young. I wanted to move on into the adventure of life. I thought it would be OK.

Friends were all around.

I remember our conversation. I'd wanted to be kind. I tried to be.

I sat with her.

I tried to be gentle.

I couldn't read her.

She just looked straight ahead.

Cold as ice.

She did that.

She never showed emotion.

She gave nothing.

I was young.

I feel terrible.

Even now feel the tension and the relief as I told her I wanted to move on. It was like that clarity in the air after a thunderstorm. I was moving to a new stage of life. I'd no idea about the lightening strike in hers.

I'm not sure that was my responsibility.

Was I so wrong?

I thought she'd get over it.

We were young.

She's right though. I was a 'selfish bastard'.

But didn't I have the right to choose?

I didn't mean to cause harm.

I wanted a clean break.

I was eighteen for God's sake.

Surely being eighteen is about fumbling and bumbling and practising for life.

I never tried to walk in her shoes, to consider how she might have felt, that she would feel.

I'm conflicted.

I was emotionally careless, naïve maybe. Surely, we can allow that in someone making sense of the world?

I can't deny, leaving her must have informed who I became; soaking me through somehow.

She's right. I can be chaotic. I work through chaos with cold, determination.

Where's that got me?

It fuelled my ambition. All around me I have its fruits. I can do some good and maybe have a little influence.

Up here in my Cupola room, in the solitude of affluence I see to the horizons of my life.

I've found my place.

I like its security.

Then again, I wonder if I blunder about and then hide up here.

I know I hide in my reserve.

It's how I present beneath my veil of propriety

Lift the veil and I'm uncertain, unsure.

Right now I feel bit of a leper clothed in rags of success, sitting on an empire of dirt.

I like that phrase 'empire of dirt'.[9] I've picked it up from the Johnny Cash's song, Hurt. I suppose he was where I am now.

It's a digression but I had a chat with Jason at the office. He told me Trent Reznor wrote Hurt.[10] I listened to him sing it. It sounds like he's caught up in obsessions. Johnny Cash sounds to be crying for redemption. The same song, differing perspectives. I'm with Johnny Cash. I've been with Trent Reznor.

I see what Pearl means!

---

[9] J. Cash - Hurt - Songwriter, T. Reznor Label, American - Lost Highway (2002)

[10] T Reznor T, - Hurt - Songwriter, T Reznor. Label, Nothing - TVT - Interscope (1995)

Day 7

I slept on it or rather tossed and turned on it, going through the motions at work. That damned letter preying on my mind.

We were teenagers.

It was half a lifetime ago.

Why does it matter so?

Deep down it matters a great deal, even though I can't see why.

It mattered then.

It matters now.

It was a small thing. It changed the course of events. Little things do.

Isn't that just life.

Isn't that teenage life?

Isn't this just dragging up the past, when the past has gone?

I've heard it said remembering makes a thing present, real again: here and now.

Is that what's happening?

A little thing released: a ghost, a shadow from the depths of who I am.

I know we're all formed by life. I'm becoming more aware of little incidents and experiences that have moulded me, the way I form relationships and doubtless how I tend to manage them.

Now that's interesting. I wrote that phrase, '*how I tend to manage them*'. That doesn't sound very nice. It's an added phrase that feels to be about control. I want to scrub it out. I don't like it. I am going to leave it where I've written it. I committed to writing and not changing anything. I'll keep that commitment.

This journal is forcing me to confront something not very nice in me?

I wonder if it does any good to let it all come to the surface?

Aren't we better letting sleeping dogs lie?

I'm obsessing.

I should stop.

Stuff is resurfacing from my mental memory box.

I'm glad I didn't read the letter when Pearl gave it to me. I would've cracked up. I can't deny it scratches at me. The ghost has become a spectre I have to call regret.

The thing is, I like that idea of living with 'no regrets'. They're like cuts covered up, regrets I mean.

It feels like I'm picking a scab on a scuffed knee. The picking seems minor. The pain is minor. The effect is minor but the scab covers healing. Pick too many times and the injury never heals.

It's a digression but I wonder why Pearl wears black with leopard print so much?

I suspect it speaks of who she is.

I'm all about who I'm supposed to be.

Deep down I've never liked feeling I'm 'supposed' to do or be anything or anyone. I know all about, 'supposed'. It fastens me to duty, like a stake in the ground.

Years ago I came across a word I've come to love: creatureliness. It's rich and pregnant with meaning, which I love. It's all about simple things: joy, pain, sorrow, fulfilment and looking beyond the tethered 'supposed'. It's about prescient hope.

I have to admit, I've never been good at this 'creatureliness'. I would love to be.

I suppose the point of this journal is to help me uncover what kind of creature I am and want to be, beneath the veneer of duty.

Day 8

My Memory box has become a Pandora's box. So the story goes, Zeus gave Pandora her box when she married his son, Epimetheus (hindsight), choosing between him and the clever Prometheus (foresight) She opened her box and the world's evils flew out: death, destruction, suffering, etc. Right at the bottom was one good thing, hope.

I'm rummaging through my life in my Memory box. I sense I'm searching for hope.

There's a picture on the lid. I think it may be mother of pearl. It's of little sailing boat in a harbour. It looks very like the jetty where Ben would tie up his barge and where I'd sit and listen to him.

The picture has a title engraved on a little brass plaque, '*Homecoming to Ithaca*'.

I've been to Ithaca.

I can't see Aunty Mary having been there. She never went anywhere. Anyway, the box is old, older than her. It's strange she'd have it.

I think it's made of walnut. The sides are somehow odd. They have a channel – a rebate – down each side.

I wonder how she came by it?

My mind is wandering from the little boat on the box lid to boats on the estuary in the fading light of the evening. I can see them through the Cupola room windows.

My fingers aimlessly play around the picture, tracing the shape of the little sailing boat.

If I remember Odysseus was taken home to Ithaca after his adventures. I've read the stories many times. Written in the iron age, I'm struck by how they speak to me.

Again I want to scrub out a phrase, 'before we'd made sense of the world'. Where did that arrogance come from; some notion people are getting better, improving? I don't think so. I suspect we're not that different.

It's interesting to think about myths and legends, but life's about hard facts: truth.

Then again, it's interesting how these myths, these stories poke through into life, beyond facts.

I noticed a photograph of me as a boy in the memory box. I'm with my grandparents. It brought a tear to my eye. It was at Michaelmas Feast. I'd be twelve or so. I'm eating fruit pie. It would be blackberry and apple. My grandmothers have posies. I will have gathered Michaelmas daisies that morning and made the posies with mum.

We don't have Michaelmas feast these days. It was in September. With Christmas, Easter, Whitsun and Halloween it marked seasons.

I feel I want to give my head a big shake. I say I prefer hard facts, yet here I am getting dreamy about festivals and traditions.

I guess they seep into your bones and give the year a certain rhythm. These days my year feels one long, bland every day.

I remember the procession from church to the menhir stones at Endymion Heights every Good Friday. I'm not sure why we called them that. We just did. It's a strange word, menhir. It means, 'long stone'. They're ancient, older than Elsternwick.

We'd meet by the lychgate for the procession and walk through the marketplace and then up Sally Lane. Then we'd go throughthrough the Sally Port and across the Stryd and from there, up the High Gate to the menhir stones.

Wonderful!

I've just remembered St John's Feast. We'd sing hymns and light a fire at the menhir stones. I've no idea why. Looking back it felt important. I have the impression it happened forever.

Memories bubbling to the surface. I'm enjoying, the memories forming and re-forming; coming alive in the present moment.

I suppose they're like buoys marking channels in the estuary, dots to join me to life.

It's a bit off the point but I went to Malta once and visited that little island in the north, I think they call it Gozo. They had an amazing feast. It seemed as if the whole island was involved.

I wonder if we've retreated behind our front doors and forgotten too much.

Day 9

I met Steve and Chris in the Ring O' Bells tonight. Sean was there. Boatman Bob sidled up and joined us.

I wish I'd kept up our sessions in the pub. It's mainly me, not Steve and Chris. They go every week.

I went tonight because I'd bumped into Steve and he reminded me about going.

Steve's to blame for this journal. He encouraged me to write it after my meltdown last year. I'd poured my heart out about what had been going on and Steve told me to 'vomit my life up' in a journal.

I've told him about Pearl and how I struggle to know what it's all about.

I never have open conversations like that.

I assume I have to live as if I've got it all worked out.

I was shocked to hear Steve's been to counselling and he'd been advised to keep his own journal. Evidently he'd had to confront a pattern of running away whenever he met someone and they'd wanted him to commit.

I don't run away. I build walls. I've always always built walls. I don't need this journal to tell me that.

I knew Steve years ago when he played for Saxby Colts. He was aways a bit of a 'Peter Perfect'. He was a good scrum half too.

Anyway, I arrived before Steve and Chris tonight. Boatman Bob was at the bar. He's a funny lad. He slid off his stool and slinked almost sideways towards me. He's a bit of a limpet but harmless enough. That said, Chris reckons there's good reason to be wary. He lives on a narrowboat at the far end of the marina.

I don't know if Chris is a bit judgemental or whether it's just that Boatman Bob doesn't fit the norm, or that maybe he is a bit dodgy.

Bob smells of oil.

His hands are never clean.

I imagine when he was a kid, he'd be the one with sticking plaster holding his spectacles together and would have his pants hanging off his arse. He has tombstone teeth, a sparse, unkempt black beard, comb-over hair and grimy hands.

Bob has a certain way when he speaks. Everything begins with a *"well uummm"* and ends with an emphatic, *"yes it is, see"*. What he says is always an interjection imposed on someone else's conversation. No. It's more an ejaculation than an interjection.

I wonder why I've written so much about Boatman Bob? Surely Chris, or more especially Steve are my actual friends and should attract more comment? Most of the time it's as if Boatman Bob burbles into his beer. Just before Chris and Steve arrived, he said something that alarmed me.

It turns out he'd seen me coming out of Scarab. - It's not far from his boat. - He didn't mention it when the others arrived. Bob said he could never go through with it. He talked about not being good at commitment.

That's the second time I've referred to commitment tonight. Maybe it's just a coincidence.

He told me he'd heard a voice the other day saying, he should stop taking his medication. I've seen him crash before. It just shows you shouldn't listen to the voices in your head! He'll crash again.

I tried to push myself away from him but Bob leaned across the table, eyes beginning to flare, hands clinging to his glass. He talked about feeling safe from *'unintended mishaps'* on his boat and that he wished he'd not come out tonight. For emphasis, he added his phrase, *'Yes it is, see'*.

He alarmed me.

I didn't look for an explanation!

Steve and Chris followed Sean in. They were half giggling with questions about my supposed 'tryst'. Chris beamed from ear to ear.

Sean is Chris's friend. I like him. He's Roman Catholic priest with chewed fingernails, spare frame and haunted eyes. He works in some grim parish in Wakefield and comes over every few weeks for respite beer. He has an emphatic, rasping Sheffield accent that makes him sound more like a foundry worker smoking sixty a day than a Parish Priest. I imagine he fits into life into life in a West Yorkshire Parish, though he does't sound the same. I don't suppose anyone outside Yorkshire would notice.

Evidently Sean had seen me with Pearl in the station cafe and told Chris.

I explained there was no 'tryst' and that we don't have any 'frisson' either.

Even writing in my journal, I feel as if I'm on my back foot, having to justify myself.

What a day for a private man! I'm spotted coming out of Scarab. I'm spotted with Pearl. Can a man have no privacy!

I might have hoped Sean would've saved the day.

I was so embarrassed. I suppose that's how it is when blokes get together. You can end up being the butt of jokes, a punchbag for a little while. It's all well-intentioned. No-one means the slightest harm. It's made me think though.

Something that on the surface was totally trivial got to me. It came from Sean. His words were a like a hot brand. He said *'Do you think it's a normal carry-on, Bran?'*, meaning me and Pearl.

I tried to defend myself.

Chris and Steve chorussed, *'the man doth protest too much!'* [11]

I'd nowhere to go.

Much beer was drunk and I had a good a time. Doubtless I'll have a banging headache in the morning.

Something occurs to me, I want to just get down on in my journal.

Steve flits from relationship to relationship, like a hummingbird moving from flower to flower. Chris is the opposite. He's rock solid. His life seems planned and ordered. Even his children have been be born to order, each one, perfect and well-scrubbed.

Perhaps I'm like Boatman Bob, chaotic and running from commitment? That's what Pearl accused me of.

I know what needs to be done and who needs to do it. It's just that sometimes I need breathing space to wait and watch.

What about Sean? Perhaps I'm more like him? He's a watcher of people. I sometimes wonder if he hides behind that dog collar.

Something he said to me ages ago has stayed with me.

---

[11] After Shakespeare W., Hamlet, Act III, Scene II

43

He told me a story about someone who'd been let down badly. He told me what he told them, '*Sometimes trust is an act of the will. Sometimes, you have to choose to trust*'.

It's stayed with me.

I find trust hard.

It's a failing.

I'm too self-contained.

I want everything framed and defined.

It's not good.

I should give myself a break every now and then.

I can see that Boatman Bob had the truth of it when he said, '*Well uummm, my old da' use' to sa', you gotta kno' yer kno'er' and that's 'bout it, as ar' sees it. Yes it is, see.*'

I might talk and talk and talk and talk and be teased mercilessly but, in the end and deep down, I '*know with my knower*'. I know what's right. I know without without words or logic or reason.

I can see that, '*comfort*' or '*frisson*' or '*tryst*' might help me know, but they're not knowing. Knowing is deeper.

I think Sean's right, you have to choose to trust and be prepared to be wrong.

I need the courage to trust what my 'knower' is saying, even though I can't explain it.

Day 10

I'm cold.

Maybe it's more that I'm remote.

It's how I come across.

It isn't how I see myself.

Inside, I'm just focused.

I don't think I'm alone in this?

This Cupola room is the place I come to find stillness, to find the singularity; the focus in me.

I like that word 'singularity'.

Maybe Pearl is right. I might be blind. I might look and not see.

I'm thinking about Boatman Bob last night. He said, 'know with your knower' but lurches from chaotic decision to chaotic decision. He doesn't seem to know his knower.

Am I any different?

I'm not Boatman Bob.

I wash in the morning for one thing.

Beyond that, maybe I'm like him.

I'm alone too.

I'm comfortable with myself. I've always been comfortable in my own skin.

It can't be about that.

I can't be just, 'knowing with your knower,' gut feeling, intuition.

Boatman Bob, muddles what he feels with what his 'knower' is telling him.

He isn't like me.

When I had my meltdown last year I couldn't think straight. I couldn't even form words. I'd sit in this chair letting my pen wander on a pad of paper. Shapes would repeat and repeat, forming themselves with no evident purpose. It seemed all random nonsense. Squiggles and patterns nothing more. I suppose it was a journal of doodling. A journal without the words.

I remember walking through town on my way for coffee and I passed some young people walking near Templar's Inn. One of them had a tattoo on the back of her neck. It was identical to one of the doodles I'd been drawing time and time again.

It's easy to pass it off as coincidence or nonsense. It's weird. I had no control of the pen as I doodled.

An even stranger thing is that the tattoo on the girl's neck and the doddle on my paper were the same as a woodcut print in Jonathan Ayton's memoir. I take it to represent his 'Labyrinth of Sorrows'. Time and again that doodle appeared from the tip of my pen, before I'd even seen the memoir.

I guess doodles come from deep inside, beyond words. Maybe they're the language of the soul spilling onto the page?

Getting doodles or words on the page brought me to a turning point.

I talked to Sean about 'turning points' one night in the Ring O' Bells. He listened. He was just quiet.

His quiet was enough.

One of the few things Sean said has played on my mind. I can hear him even now. I don't know if he said it just the once, but words have echoed in my mind. He said, 'Go home, Bran'. I was pissed that night. There's no getting away from it. Whatever he meant, the phrase lodged in my brain.

Last year, Father Francis wrote to me out of the blue. It wasn't long after I'd talked to Sean. He invited me over to the Queens in Elsternwick. I went to be polite but I had to confront so many demons, Pearl being one. I'd not imagined I would see her and certainly not pissed or dressed like a hooker.

I couldn't face the drive home that night. Instead I walked right up the High Gate to the menhir stones at Endymion Heights. I wanted to get away from everyone and everything to just think; or rather try to let my mind go blank and not think.

I sheltered under the blackthorn by the pinfold. It was always somewhere I'd go to get away. Life hit me like an express train. Thoughts and emotions collided. What Pearl said that night made it worse.

I slept up there all night.

I dreamed.

In my dream I climbed the same High Gate path, this time with a spectre at my heels. Rain and wind slashed and cut me so hard blood specks peppered me. I remember the terror. Everything was black except the spectre and their crimson cloak, flapping about, compounding the terror; lunging at me with long; grasping fingers reaching grab me.

It was awful.

I remember I waking under the blackthorn disorientated and terrified as my past collided with my present.

I'm coming to realise, we stumble and fall through life making the best.

The challenge seems to be having the wherewithal of get back up and keep going.

It can be bloody hard!

Day 11

I'm sitting in a pool of light from a little lamp by my chair. The darkness surrounding me compounds my solitude. The cosmos is spinning above my head, projected on the Cupola ceiling.

I'm looking into the night covering the estuary. Lights pepper the dark waters from boats and from buoys marking safe channels.

It feels as if there's no-one else.

I'm the only one.

The CD playing in my darkness was on the doormat when I arrived home. There's a thread running through the songs.

These words haunt me:
"There's a light and I can see it in your eyes
There's a memory of the way you used to be" [12]

I've been relaxing, taking in the night sky on the cupola ceiling. I love the feeling I'm at one with the universe.

Concentrating on the Pole Star, constant in the night sky spotting constellations, pictures from connected stars. I track along the tail of Little Bear, Ursa Minor and across the night from the Pole Star to Ursa Major - the Great Bear.

It never ceases to amaze me that from the time people first settled here, they've looked up and seen these two bears in the night sky. I suppose it's the story the Greeks told that most remember. Many other stories are older, far older. I like the Greek one. If I remember, it goes something like this:

Zeus had an affair with a pretty girl called Callisto. She swore a vow of chastity she broke having child to Zeus. She called him Arcas. Zeus' jealous wife cursed Callisto turning her into a bear.

As the story goes, when Arcas had grown, he went hunting and prepared to kill the bear that was really Callisto. Evidently Zeus was keeping watch and turned Arcas into a bear. He then picked Callisto and Arcas up by their tails and hurled them into the night sky. Arcas became the Little Bear. Callisto the Great Bear. So they were protected from harm but banished from the world, there constellations never touching the horizon.

---

12 S Ryder - Stompa - Songwriters, S Ryder & J Bettis Label, EMI Capitol (2012)

Arcas couldn't help who he was any more than I can help who I am.

Arcas and Callisto are a myth, presenting truth so it might be found.

I'm such a nerd. I'm sitting here thinking about other stories, other myths that help me feel for truth in the darkness.

They're all around, I guess. I suppose this is where you have to go with your knower, I mean 'know with your knower'. That's what Boatman Bob says anyway.

I've just remembered where my fascination with the Arcas of the Greeks began.

There's that wall of mirrors in the White Sitting Room of the Dower House. I remember being fascinated by it. I used to go to Sunday afternoon parties at the Dower House as a boy. The mirrors were at one end of the White Sitting Room. At the other end was a wall of windows onto the garden. The mirrors were framed with a plaster frieze telling the story of Arcas and Callisto. It hemmed in reflections of real people. Thinking about it, the mirrors contained real life within the myth, fixing them together for a moment.

The dowager, Lady Gwyneth loved her parties in the White Sitting Room. With the craggiest, old lady face and worn out twinset, her eyes would laugh with the spirit of a teenager. I don't know if she's still alive. Cora was her companion. Now she was an interesting woman!

I've always wanted to break out of the story, to break out of the frame.

I'm staring at the Pole Star, up there on my cupola ceiling. It's fixed and constant. Navigators find their way by it.

If that fixed point disappears there's no reference. Direction is lost.

Deep down I know that in my life, I lost sight of the Pole Star, lost direction.

I've lost my way.

I've been drifting for years.

The words of that song are playing in my mind. It feels like some kind of siren call. Does a siren call to save, or to warn, or misdirect?

God, this is deep!

Day 12

I wrote about 'Old Mother Riley' today. Her family wanted me to give a eulogy at her funeral. I can't make it. I've written something to be read by someone else. It's more an obituary than a eulogy. I'm splitting hairs. Writing brought memories to the surface.

It seems right to remember 'Old Mother Riley' in my journal.

It's funny how I gave her that name. It was just something between she and I (or is it, her and me?) I doubt anyone else called her that.

My grandparents loved to watch Saturday afternoon films in black and white on a little TV in their kitchen. Sometimes I'd watch with them. One of the characters in the films made me laugh. I haven't a clue about their real name. It was a man playing a washer-woman called 'Old Mother Riley'. I gave Jean that name. I don't know why.

My 'Old Mother Riley' had twinkling eyes and a smile that knew every nuance of who I was. The phrase 'Yes love', was her constant, emphatic affirmation. She encouraged endlessly, not in the detail but of the person. I'll never forget her.

I wrote this about her:

> It is rare to meet someone for whom warmth and generous humour is their natural state.
>
> As many time-served members of St John's might know, to me Jean was 'Old Mother Riley'. I learned a huge amount from her about the kind of person I would want to be. I learned from the kind of person she was: full of warmth, generosity and acceptance.
>
> For me, Old Mother Riley leaked love.
>
> Her's wasn't limp love some might occasionally be guilty of, with warm words and a bitter heart. Her's wasn't lace doily and delicate, teacup love. It was the pot 'o tea love that said, 'I will be here in spite of what's going on and in spite what might have happened'.
>
> These days, at every turn we are taught to laud the creative, successful genius, the self-made entrepreneur, the person who excels in whatever way. Yet it seems to me that 'Old Mother Riley's' quality of life looked in the opposite direction. It seems to me her humility and generosity meant that somehow she saw all she had as borrowed rags. I suspect that even her reflection in the mirror was, as C. S. Lewis put it, 'an image that is not

ours[13], *that is not her own. I think she saw that same image in those around her.*

There is no great mystery in this. I think 'Old Mother Riley' simply looked beyond herself and looked to the goodness in others. In fact I think she learned about this goodness by seeing it in others and through seeking it for herself.

I'm not sure I've always put what I learned from her into practice. I know sometimes I've gone in exactly the opposite direction to her, thinking my destiny might lie in my own adventures, my own independence.

I suspect Old Mother Riley would just smile, say, 'Yes love,' supporting me, the person but showing me the way she knew.

I meant every word. It's not how she might have seen herself.

I suppose what really matters isn't dry facts, dates and events. They're just markers and milestones, revealing the path we've taken in life. We might show off about them or regret them. What matters is something different. I guess it's the connections we have with people in the stories, myths and the texture of relationships the matter most.

It's funny, I've not thought like this before and I've certainly not thought about 'Old Mother Riley' like this. I've never really considered the influence she's been and I've certainly not stopped to think about this business of how I see.

[13] C.S. Lewis, "Christianity and Literature" in *Christian Reflections*, Walter Hooper (1967) p. 7

Day 13

The man I met today had his head on upside down. It was a shiny bald head with a thick black hipster beard. He was older than a hipster, although I'm not sure how old hipsters are. Anyway, he wasn't wearing a checked shirt.

His eyes sparkled violence, beneath thick, dark brows. He was a paradox of menacing violence mingled with human interest.

I liked him.

He turned out to be kind and thoughtful and not at all how he looked to me.

We had a conversation about fear and hope.

He liked his idea that fear is the absence of direction and hope is the opposite, the means of direction.

I like that very much.

Whilst my intuition was that he might be kind, his violence was palpable.

I didn't like that.

He stirred a memory of David.

David shot me in the knee with an airgun when I was standing at the bus stop. I can hear him laughing with his big, wide, loud mouth and cackling laugh. His laugh hurt more than the airgun pellet.

I'm not sure why the man I met today reminded me of David.

I know I wrote about Old Mother Riley's twinkling eyes yesterday and how they were full of warmth. How is it I saw violence in this man's twinkling eyes?

David was a long time ago.

It's strange how that memory hurts.

After I'd seen the man with the upside down head, I went to see mum and other memories surfaced.

We had to face the worst.

I remember the last time this happened.

Then she had visits from the church's paramilitary ladies - the Mother's Union - with set hair and tweed skirts. They drank tea and ate madeira cake in the drawing room and brought Sombre Sympathy with them. I wrote that as a proper noun. It felt like a real thing. They left Sombre Sympathy in the drawing room. It lingered along with their 'Lily of the Valley'.

I'm sure they'd intended to bring hope.

She didn't die as they predicted.

She's in a living death now.

The first death I met was Austin's.

Tom and I heard the news together.

We were boys.

Just fifteen.

We'd been with him a few days earlier.

He'd shown us his new guitar.

He was a natural. He didn't have to think about it. He and Martin played together. I had to practise and practise with mine and didn't get far.

I know its a digression, but I always said I'd let my thoughts fall onto the page. This one feels important. I wrote practise, with an 's' and not practice with a 'c'. These days, people just write practice, with a 'c'. I like the distinction of the 's': a verb and all about action. It's a noun with a 'c'. PractiCe to something, an object, a thing. It might seem like nothing but 'practiSe' is about doing.

I know there is that other form with a 'c', which is to do with effort and habit, but that's still describing something. I like the idea of getting wrapped up in doing.

I like to be clear, even for myself.

Death takes practise, by which I mean action, something happening.

Austin died. He was just a boy.

It feels unfair.

54

Life's not about fair.

Other things are about fair.

We have to work at what's fair.

We have to practise and work hard at it.

As a teenager, I practised with Deb. That was intense. Immersive!

Then there was Pearl.

She took me to her house just once. She showed me her bedroom. I remember the wallpaper. It had little green and pink flowers. Standing in her bedroom doorway, I wanted to go in, I felt I shouldn't. I've no idea why. It didn't feel right.

It's a strange thing, because I'd no qualms about going up to the pinfold with Janet Field. We'd have a fumble and a grope, under the Blackthorn tree.

It didn't feel right going into Pearl's bedroom. I don't know why.

We danced a distant dance she and I. In step but never touching. I don't think anyone else would see it this way but somehow she was too delicate. I could never say that to her. She's more fragile than she lets on.

Writing this journal is such a strange experience. I'm beginning to explore the way I see things, even small things and the way they affect me.

It's good. I'm finding fresh perspective, another way of seeing.

I'm thinking about the dining room mirror when I was growing up. It was on the wall, behind the table. It had a border of fluted glass that spun rainbow sunlight streamed through the french windows. The mirror was tinted the faintest pink. Mum said it made you look healthy.

Mum looks in a different mirror on a different wall now. It's sterile, plain glass. I'm not sure who she sees.

I think about losing her.

It's at such times, alone feels like abandoned.

It's the root of my fear: being abandoned and lost in Alone.

I can imagine it to be a place, Alone.

I imagine it's like being without hope, lost in dark waters with no light.

I suppose fear is not knowing the right direction more than the dark waters or the darkness.

Mum is alive.

I was there when dad died.

'Beautiful' is the best word I have for the experience of being with him. It's the only word.

I was at the foot of his bed. He looked at me: brown eyes looking out from the blurred edge between life and not life. Love passed through the blur and back again.

Beautiful feels a strange way to describe my dad dying. It was just that.

He saw his son in that moment. I saw my dad.

I want to look into my own mirror and see the son dad saw.

I want dad's hope for me.

I want it very much

All I see is middle-aged reality in a lonely mirror.

I look in the bathroom mirror in the morning, face squashed and creased from sleep, eyes sagging with bleary bags, hair raggedy and grey stubble. I scrape my face with a razor and shower with the same routines. I mark the same number of footsteps to the bathroom; then to the closet for that white shirt, those black jeans; then to the kitchen for the same coffee, day in and day out.

I look in the hall mirror before I step out to the face the day. I brush my hair in the same way, cover my head in my habitual fedora and take up the walking stick others see as eccentric and I see as sentimental.

Day by day, the habits roll on and on and on, repeating on and on and on. There's no direction in this, except within the maelstrom of convention that's sucked me in.

Actually, that's not true.

There's been one change.

There's the scarf Pearl left in the station cafe. It hangs over the corner of the mirror, waiting for me to give it back. I touch it and am tempted to put it in my satchel each morning.

From now on, I think I will. It can be a new part of my morning. A gesture, nothing more.

I'll have a part of her with me.

Day 14

I've been standing by the window of the Cupola room watching squalls of rain blow in from the estuary and make rat-tat splashes on the windows.

I like the feel of the sculptures I keep by the window. They're alabaster. Viv made them. I love her work. They're about being born. Raw and rough at the base, graceful spirits are reaching up and out of the rock.

The names were her idea. She called them Juno and Ceres and carved their names without asking. She told me, 'The stones became these spirits'.

It annoyed me.

I didn't say.

I'm in my chair writing this.

I could've stayed by the window.

My mind finds itself with dad.

He was the opposite of alabaster grace.

He was consistency, propriety and order.

Earlier today I was looking at his medals in the Memory box. With them is a little cloth badge. It's faded and tatty.

There's a motto embroidered round the edge: *Honi soit qui mal y pense*. I know what it means: *"Shame upon him who thinks evil of it"*. It's the motto of the Blues and Royals. Dad taught me that. He said it was their nickname. It's seems odd a regiment might have a nickname. I'm not sure quite how it worked. He said the Blues came from the Parliamentarians and the Royals from the Royalists after the civil wars.

Dad gave me his medals and this badge for my Memory box after I'd been rummaging in an old suitcase in the attic. I found them with two books. One was about el Alamein. I can't remember the other, except it was about adventures........Burnaby I think his name was. It was called, A Ride to Khiva.

Dad found me reading in my bedroom, his medals laid out round me. He never talked about the war. All I know is he was a Major and Casey was his Batman.

Casey was dark.

He was Market Constable and did dad's bidding, carrying that walking stick made of elm with a huge, bulbous end as a badge of office. It was more a cudgel than a walking stick.

I could never have lived to dad's standards.

I wonder if Nathaniel Ayton thought that of Jonathan? Jonathan would've been High Steward, like dad. Nathaniel must've followed him. That's how it works, father to son.

Dad wanted it for me. He never said.

I wonder what dad would've written about his life? I wonder what he'd have written about me? I wonder if he'd have been proud?

I ran into Carolyn in Saxby. I hadn't seen her since the old days in Elsternwick. We had a chat about the new jacket I've just bought. As we exchanged goodbyes she said, 'Remember to try new things on to see what fits, Bran.' I'm not sure she meant my jacket.

When I was maybe seventeen or eighteen, she and I went for a drink. I thought all my birthdays had come at once! She picked me up in a bright blue Ford Mustang. Carolyn was well above my pay grade. It turned out she was worried about me and Debs, with her blond hair, apple cheek freshness and sparkling blue eyes. She looked me straight in the eye and said 'Bran, Miss Debs isn't right for you'. I can hear her say it and I can see the look on her face; bright green, happy eyes suddenly serious. She was right.

Just how do we know what's right? It's all very well Boatman Bob saying, 'you have to know with your knower'.

What happens if we believe in our heart something's right but the world says otherwise.

What happens if we know with our knower and hold off taking action.

I do that.

I can see Pearl does it.

She signals one thing and throws up a barrier.

Am I any different.

We dance to the same beat, never dancing together.

That's how it feels.

Then again I remember Sean's words in the pub. He said, *'Do you think that's a normal carry-on, Bran?'.* I know what he meant.

From the privacy of this journal, I know I protest too much. I retreat to, 'comfortable'.

How do I reach beyond comfortable? ,

It was Pearl who said 'comfortable' first.

It's her word.

It's set the boundary. That's how it feels, a boundary. A boundary to what? It's not like me, but I don't know.

I'm just pondering Juno and Ceres, graceful spirits emerging into alabaster purity. I wonder if their siren's calls are louder or closer? I just don't know. All I know is that I have to accept what is, irrespective of.........

.........I'm not sure what the irrespective is, or might be...........

.............what is comfortable.

I feel comfortable.

It's not a word - a concept - I've used much in life up to now.

I may be deluded.

I'm going with it and trying not to over-think.

Day 15

A lovely invitation was waiting for me when I got home. It was from Tess. I'm very touched, but left with a challenge.

I want to accept.

I'm not sure I should.

I'm not sure it's appropriate.

I'm twice her age.

It's all very well meeting when she's in town, but staying over for the weekend is a big step.

I know I can be an arse and shouldn't be so concerned about the way things look. I am though.

I'm tempted.

She's very lovely.

We have a 'connection'.

It's not like the connection with Pearl but 'connection' is the only word I have.

I wish I knew what these connections are!

I've just remembered about something Sheila, my PA says. She reckons every relationship is sexual to some extent. I've never felt comfortable with that notion. It makes no sense. Mind you, Shiela's a shagger. People smirk about her exploits. She's had affairs all over the place. At work, you'd think butter wouldn't melt in her mouth!

I can't reduce every relationship to a sexual transaction. It's an appalling idea.

I don't want there to be a connection with Tess if it's sexual. I just like her company.

I confess, if I was twenty years younger I might think differently. She's certainly the kind of girl I would've been attracted to but that's it. There's nothing sexual in my connection. I'd hate it if there was.

I'm just thinking about one of Steve's old girlfriends. She was old enough to be his daughter. Steve told me he'd met her father and he was not far off his own age. I wonder how that all worked.

I once saw some TV sketch show where they took the piss out of a bloke who'd picked up a girl old enough to be his daughter and the girl was fleecing him.

It's no better than whoring, reducing everything to a sexual transaction. It's not appropriate. It's not right. I'd hate that.

Maybe I'm naive.

Pearl said she thought I was blind.

I hate seedy and salacious. It makes relationships seem no better than paying a hooker for a shag. I've never done that, nor would I.

Anyway, with Tess, we hit it off from the moment she pulled a pint for me in the Queens when I had that meal with Father Francis last year.

I'm glad she got in touch.

I like having lunch with her every now and then.

She likes books and I like books. It's refreshing, spending time with her.

I'm surprised I wrote the phrase 'It's refreshing'. It felt right.

It's funny, as I wrote it I could taste the sour-sweet taste of sherbet in my mouth. What was that about, except I'm making a connection to 'refreshing'. Isn't it a weird thing, how these powerful association are made.

Tess and I read Sir Gawain and the Green Knight together. I'd read it before. In fact, I suggested it to her.

In the past Carolyn has poked the odd jibe at me. She'd say, *'that wasn't very chivalrous, Sir Gawain'*.

Anyway, I like it as a book.

Tess teased me about Sir Gawain last time she and I met. She quoted this at me:
The chief thing praised in all of chivalry is the royal sport of love.[14]

---

[14] Translated by J. R. R. Tolkien. Sir Gawain And the Green Knight, Pearl, and Sir Orfeo. London :Allen & Unwin, (1975)

64

She's picked up that I dance around the edges of love, looking in, never speaking of it.

You'd have thought I'd got it sussed at my age, but no.

There's enough distance between us, for Tess to tease.

It'll be a wholly different thing, going to stay with her.

I have to keep in my mind that she's inviting me because of the gig at the Queens this weekend. I'm sure that's the only reason. She's being thoughtful and has invited me because Martin's band is playing and I've told her I'd like to hear them.

Martin used to love John Fogerty, I imagine they'll play Credence.

I'm going to just go with it and try not to 'over-think'.

I can't help feeling conflicted but her invitation has made me happy.

Is that wrong?

I'm not sure how others will see things.

It bothers me.

I'm over-thinking. I know I am.

I've told her about this journal. Evidently she's intrigued and says she senses I obsess in this Cupola room and need to get out. I'm sure she's right.

Tess told me she's kept her own diary for years, going back to being a child in Cambridge. She told me she'd go to the Botanic Gardens and write. I know the gardens well. I can picture her there.

I imagine her sitting in the sunshine writing and maybe wandering round the Glasshouse Range. That's my favourite part.

I am settled to the idea of going.

It will be good.

Day 16

Walking through the front door this evening, I was reminded of the day I began this journal. I remember commenting on how I liked that solid thus far and no further clunk as the door closed and I hung up my jacket and fedora and put my walking stick in the stand. Now I also take Pearl's scarf out of my satchel and hang it over the corner of the mirror.

I've been carrying Pearl's letter round in my jacket pocket since the day I read it.

As I hung my jacket up, I took the letter out to re-read before putting it in my Memory box. Holding it gave me a deep, pit-of-the-stomach feeling of, well I'm not sure whether to write excitement or anxiety.

I can have such a storm of conflicting emotions these days. It's really not like me.

In fact before I came up here to write, I stood in front of the hall mirror and had a feeling more like rage as I looked at my reflection.

No. 'Rage' isn't quite right.

It was more resentment at the man I saw in the mirror. I don't know where the feeling came from.

I wanted to bellow 'fuck off' at that man in the mirror. So I did.

It felt so good, I did it again and again and then again.

I caught sight another reflection: the girl in the painting behind me. I could've sworn I caught her smiling. I'm convinced she smiled. I know it's ridiculous to even think that. The reality is, it's only an impression of a girl anyway. Yet in my mind she smiled.

Anyway amongst this tumble of emotions, I quite like the idea of clinging to excitement.

In fact, I sense a growing......I'm not sure what.......maybe confidence. I'm not sure that's it. I'm struggling for a word. Perhaps the word 'presence' just about does it. I like that word. It fits. I'm not convinced what I mean by it, but I like it.

Sometimes words aren't enough. Maybe we should give up on them. I'm not sure they're what matters most.

Anyway I'm in my chair in the Cupola room. The Memory box is on my lap. I'm going to put Pearl's letter in there.

I've been distracted rummaging and found myself quite taken by the bit of old hinge, along with that big old key. I've no idea why I never threw them out. The hinge has a very rustic feel. I could imagine some village blacksmith knocking it up. I wonder where it came from? As to the key, it's a smaller version of those you see in the locks on very old doors. It has that tatty cloth tag on it. I suppose I just took the box as Aunty Mary gave it to me and didn't throw away what came with it.

It's a shame Pearl won't be there over the weekend. She can't help having to go to Selwyn again. Perhaps it's just as well.

I took another look at that letter before I put it in the Memory box. She certainly knows how to make a point!

> *'Clean, ordered, self-contained, successful Bran. You left me in chaos and thought it OK. You bastard.*
>
> *You are blind*
>
> *You think you are one thing but you are another. You think you are in control but you are out of control. You live a fairyland reality. You are a lie, a deception.'*

My whole adult life, I've not been bothered if someone didn't like what I might do or say. You can't be liked by everyone. I remember that fool of a man - who's name I won't even record - who dismissed me saying I had a 'mixed press'. It was just the power-play of a weak man. Who wants to be a vanilla no-body or some sycophant with a tidy desk, a habit of grandstanding a morality you don't live up to and a greasy pole to climb?

He turned out a puffed up liar. He made clear his public disdain for dishonestly then chose to lie, using lawyers to underline his hypocrisy. I think he's angling for another high profile job. It sickens me. Ambition has overtaken integrity. That's always dangerous.

Anyway, I have all the files in my safe. He's corrupt. I'm tempted to out him. I'm sure I will in the end. It's only right.

Anyway what Pearl wrote got to me. Her's weren't a weak, foolish, dishonest sycophant's words. She wrote about me, the person inside.

It's disconcerting that I've failed to see.

I've been blind to so much.

I suppose only someone like Pearl would make me look.

I suppose standing in front of the hall mirror and shouting 'fuck off' was about being honest about myself. It's funny - frightening - how we get stuck behind impressions of ourselves and start to believe them.

Of course I know I have to present myself to the world. I have to get along with others. I can't just do what I want.

Something occurs to me that helps me make sense. It's just a detail.

She wore that leopard print scarf when we met the other day. She always wears leopard print. It might be shoes, or a handbag or a scarf, whatever. It's a motif, wherever she is.

I suppose I have my motifs, little symbols that speak volumes. I wonder what they say about me?

I need to think about this when I go to Elsternwick tomorrow.

I'll take my journal with me. I'm not sure I'll get time to write but I'll try. In fact, I'll promise myself to write something each day, come what may.

Day 17

I'm sitting in a cafe in North Bar, opposite St John's. It seems to be run by tattooed hipsters. The one who served me suggested lemon might spoil my earl grey. It is excellent without.

This cafe used to be a bank. It's part of a Georgian terrace stretching from the medieval North Bar gate to the marketplace. I think there were other buildings here before that. I imagine they were destroyed in Lilburne's siege.

They've kept the the bank's motto over the fireplace:
  Viam prudentiae ostendit [15]

I remember, the bank had a uniformed commissionaire. Mr Hetherington with his brass buttons and a black uniform. He was verger at St John's and had one arm and a limp.

Grandma called him, 'lame'.

We're not allowed to call anyone lame now.

We say 'disabled'.

I know from work, we have to take all 'reasonable and proportionate' steps to make buildings accessible, creating opportunities for people with disabilities. I've done the training. I wasn't convinced. I'm not sure the difference between 'able' and 'disable(ed)' is binary. Anyway, I wonder who really decides?

I'm not sure Mr Hetherington would've thought of himself as disabled.

He was 'able'. It's just that he had one arm and a limp. He was lame. It didn't matter.

'Lame' was descriptive not discriminatory.

Mr. Hetherington was in the war. He commanded respect.

Mr. Ormerod was the bank's manager when I was young. He lived not far from us. I remember his fantastic cream Rover 3.5 V8. A dream car. He had a bald head that twitched for no obvious reason. He'd hold it slightly on one side all the time, as if he had a permanent crick in his neck. He'd been something in the war too.

---

[15] Prudence Shows the Way

Mr Ormerod sang bass in the church choir. I sat across the chancel from him. His eyes seemed to pop out and almost explode as he sang. What with his eyes and twitching head, it was difficult not to laugh.

He was nice to me. He took a belt to Simon.

There were those stories of how he'd meet all the new recruits and buy them a cup of tea and an iced bun. The girls used to say he'd just happen to squeeze past them in the stationery cupboard, even though he had a secretary. I seem to remember one girl telling me how he had her go round to his side of the desk and sit on his knee to take notes from him. I suppose it was just accepted back then.

My mind is wandering around the motto on the fireplace. It means 'Prudence Shows the Way'. I suppose the intended inference might be that prudence means 'caution' or 'care'. I hope it was more about making wise decisions, knowing the right thing to do. The bank's motto is really, 'Know the Right Thing to Do'.

I wonder if it was 'right' to turn the bank into a café? It's a far cry from Mr Hetherington's polished brass buttons.

There are posters on the wall about taking risks.

Dad always wanted me to take risks, to find courage and have an adventure.

I especially like these sayings on the posters:

> *'Only those who risk going too far can possibly find out how far they can go'.*

> *'In the end we only regret the chances we didn't take'.*

I like this one from Mohammed Ali

> *'He who is not courageous enough to take risks will accomplish nothing in life'.*

Most of the tables are filled with people wearing headphones. I've no idea if they've read the posters.

No one speaks, at least not to anyone else in the cafe.

Grey haired men are hovering uncomfortably around the edges of the cafe in bright purple t-shirts. I notice, they have the word 'mentor' stamped across their backs. I half recognise one of them. I'm sure we were at school together.

The leaflet on the table tells me the café is a social enterprise and business incubator for digital entrepreneurs. I guess the people in the bright purple t-shirts are mentoring the hipster, digital entrepreneurs. Interesting!

I'm not sure how years spent wearing a grey suit, growing grey hair and working in a bank qualifies you as a mentor. I suppose it keeps them off the streets and does no harm, even if it creates no benefit.

It turns out a woman called Louise manages the cafe. She has a broad smile, over-sized glasses and a squint. I like her. She was neither digital hipster nor a grey-suited mentor in a purple t-shirt.

I'm reminded of Stuart who I met in his club in Mayfair. He was something in the dot.com bubble. We talked about warehouses in Shoreditch and how graduates with names like Julian and Jasper sat at wooden benches with MacBooks and called themselves Technology Entrepreneurs.

Anyway, the cafe's tea and cake are very good. My cake is Polenta and Orange. There wasn't Polenta in Elsternwick when I was growing up.

I wonder what happened to Mr. Hetherington and Mr. Ormerod.

With no sense of purpose, my gaze wandered out of the window, finding its way across the marketplace to the Elstern bridge, with its victorian mock towers and portcullis gates.

My mind joined my gaze and thought about the bridge. It seems a crazy thing to build in a town like Elsternwick. It's like a mini London, Tower Bridge. There's an inscription on each tower. They've always struck a chord with me. On the East Tower, it reads, *'Fear not for the future'*, on the West Tower the inscription reads *'Weep not for the past'*.[16]

I'd better stop writing now. I can see Tess walking across the marketplace. She has something of a nymph about her with that mass of ash blond hair. She reminds me of the girl in the painting in my hall.

[16] Percy Bysshe Shelley, Queen Mab, W Clark (1821)

Day 18

Tess has brought me to her apartment. It's just along the terrace from the cafe that was a bank.

I keep telling myself it's OK but worry how things might look. It feels slightly inappropriate to be here. Yet we share a fondness I value.

What a stupid, forced expression, 'we share a fondness I value'. I'm such an arse.

Someone once described me as 'a fart in a wetsuit'. I own that!

I'm writing this in Tess's spare room. There's a bed and a little chair and not much more. It's enough.

Straining to look out of the tiny window, I can just see the estuary glistening silver-grey in the distance as well as the tops of the towers on Elstern Bridge, the way back along the coast road to Saxby.

I'm thinking about my drive along that bleak road today with its marshy ings on one side and shifting sands on the other.

I stopped at the Look Out on my way here. It looks over the ings and sands. On tourist maps, it's marked as a 'viewing point' now. I thought about the story I learned as a boy about Christopher Fleet luring the vanguard of Lilburne's army into the sands and then lighting a beacon on the Look Out to warn the town the army would be coming.

As children, we were warned about the sands and what were called Secret Ways, the ways Christopher Fleet knew.

I saw an expanse of sand along the Fylde coast on the TV not long ago. A presenter was standing in the wet sands, sinking. She did it on purpose. A rescue team was on hand.

As she moved, her feet, back and forth she sank further and further in. She tried to pull her feet out but just sank deeper and deeper. With every movement she was drawn further in.

The tide was a threat. It was coming in and would engulf her. She was like a statue with a forced smile for the television and arms outstretched for balance.

At the mercy of the creeping tide and sucking sands, water trickled about her boots drawing them deeper into the sand.

Even with safe hands to rescue, there was fear in her eyes and in her voice.

Fear drew her in as much as the sand and water.

Arms reached in and pulled her to safety, leaving her boots behind. Sand and water claimed them.

It was no joke.

It was staged but real.

I wonder how she felt.

I wonder how it felt: trapped, then clasped; embraced and then pulled out?

There will have been people watching nearby. I was watching. She had people looking to her safety. I wonder how they felt watching the creeping tide draw her in.

It was just a stunt.

Entertainment.

Danger played with.

There was no risk.

Entertainment is about becoming part of what's going on, almost.

It's about empathy.

Empathy isn't over there watching. Empathy is standing on the sand.

Looking out of the window of Tess's flat, I realise I've watched the world from the window of my Cupola room and observed with disinterested sympathy. I looked on from a distance. That's not empathy.

The gentle knock at the door is calling me. I'm looking forward to hearing what Tess has to say, to finding out more about why she came to Elsternwick.

Day 19

Her sitting room is small.

There's a tiny kitchen at one end.

It's a cook's kitchen, filled with Italy.

She'd made pesto, which surprised me. I don't know why it should surprise me.

Traces of Tess's life were spread around.

She has a great many books. I'm not surprised. I don't know why I'm not surprised.

The room was full of the disarray of someone at ease with themselves. I've aspired to disarray all my life.

She has a banjo. I'm surprised by that too. Again, I don't know why.

There's a poem on the wall. It's handwritten and framed. I know it, but not by heart.

I've copied it out:
> To suffer woes which Hope thinks Infinite;
> To forgive wrongers darker than the death of night;
> To defy Power, which seems omnipotent;
> To love, and to bear; to Hope until Hope creates;
> From its own wreck the thing it contemplates;
> Neither to change, nor falter, nor repent;
> This, like thy glory, Titan, is to be
> Good, great and joyous, beautiful and free.
> This is alone Life, Fly, Empire and Victory.[17]

The words confront me. I receive them as a call to defiance: to break bonds, to find hope.

It's funny, I wonder if so much I've come to hold dear is more like a binding, a tying down.

It's lovely here.

When we sat down to eat she flaked white truffle over scrambled eggs and brought the plates to the table with truffle oil.

---

[17] Percy Bysshe Shelley, Prometheus Unbound, (1820)

I wonder if she knew?

How could she know about this exact meal?

I've never told her.

How could I have told her.

It was perfect.

Every mouthful, ecstasy.

To my endless embarrassment I ate silently; contained in pleasure.

I saw delight in her grey eyes.

There was no awkwardness.

This also surprised me.

I should I have felt awkward!

I believe I should.

We had linguine run through with fresh pesto after the scrambled eggs.

I knew it would be a nightmare for my shirt.

It was.

I tried not to fuss.

She'd made a salad: anchovies, quail eggs and parmesan to go with the pasta.

Tess knows how to cook!

The chatter was light: of Rome and Umbria and Cambridge and Elsternwick and life.

I told her about the drive from Saxby to Elsternwick.

I talked about the presenter on the Fylde coast in the television programme.

She laughed.

Tess laughed, telling me, 'It's not Fylde. It's Flyde'.

She giggled.

I was embarrassed and must have shown it because she said very gently, 'Yes, honestly, it is Flyde'.

There was warmth in her voice and a generous smile.

To try and recover the situation, I said, 'oh you mean like flied'.

I always think you say 'Fylde' as in filed.

We laughed.

We joked about Fylde and filed and Flyde and flied. It was nothing really, a talking point, the swapping of a letter. It didn't change the meaning. It didn't change the place. Whether Flyde of Fylde, the place was the same.

I'll remember tonight for a very long time.

In the moment my shirt distracts me. It's peppered with green and oil. I'm embarrassed but relaxed.

Taking to my bed a simple thought is in my head, 'why a banjo'?

Day 20

She knocked on my bedroom door. It's much later than I'd normally be up.

I sat on the edge of my bed with memories from last night coming to mind.

I smiled, dressed and opened the door to find strong, black coffee on a little tray outside the door.

Unsure of the protocol and anxious not to trespass on her hospitality, I was keen to leave her apartment discreetly. Prying eyes might think something improper had been going on.

I could hardly wear a placard saying, 'I stayed in the spare room'.

I worry about life's detail.

It's just how I am.

I deserve that description, 'a fart in a wetsuit'.

Anyway, Tess had laid the table for breakfast: orange juice, toast and more coffee.

She seemed pensive, rocking back slightly in her chair.

Her fingers drummed on the table while the jam pot held her attention.

She spoke in a vacant, not quite in the room way.

All the while she drummed and focussed on the jam pot.

I began to wish I hadn't come and that I might go away.

With trepidation, I said, 'Go on?'

I had to coax her but was unsure.

She recalled the evening we first met, explaining how she'd come home and looked through old photographs in a wooden box she'd been given.

I asked her to show me.

She found the box under a pile of papers and passed it to me. It was more or less identical to my own memory box. Like mine, hers had a beautiful mother of pearl inlay in the lid and a label The label read, 'Persephone's Redemption'. It's a picture of a beautiful woman surrounded by what looks like grain and fruit and clutching a box.

She told me her box had always been in the family, as far as she knew and that it had been given to her as a sign of growing up. Again, a connection.

She asked a question from nowhere, 'What brought you back to Elsternwick?'

My answer was simple. I told her Father Francis had invited me last year and I felt it discourteous not to accept.

I asked her if she knew the inscriptions on the Elstern Bridge and explained I'd tried to live them as a motto and that I'd left as soon as I could.

She pressed her point, 'So why come back?'

I repeated, it was because Father Francis invited me and that I had simply been polite.

She pressed her point. 'Why are you here now?'

My only answer was, 'Because you invited me'.

As I sit here writing this, it still feels right I've come. It's a gut feeling it's right. I'm not questioning it.

She looked straight at me and said, 'You've been blown home, haven't you'.

I tried to hide behind my coffee cup.

I wanted to gather my thoughts.

I'd wanted my thoughts to be simpler.

I wanted my thoughts to be about visiting Elsternwick, because I'd been invited.

All I could say was an involuntary, 'Yes'.

There was silence.

She opened her box, rummaged through and passed me a photograph. It was of me on the ruins of the castle's curtain wall wearing those red trousers I loved. I can't remember why I stopped wearing red trousers.

She rummaged again and pulled out a key saying, 'any ideas.........?'

82

I just said, 'I haven't a clue'. The words just came out, I know there was the chill of dismissal in my tone she didn't deserve. I certainly haven't a clue where that came from.

The exchange between us played on my mind as I prepared for my morning.

Day 21

I'm back in the café.

I wandered round Elsternwick this morning and called in at St John's on my way to the marketplace.

I'd fancied a bit of a walk so went via Hag's Wynd.

It's a nice walk, although it used to give me the creeps as a young lad.

There was nothing creepy this morning.

Sunlight streamed through the trees.

I heard Hag's Force tumbling water over the rocks in the river down the steep rhododendron covered bank to the right of the path. I hate rhododendrons. We all have likes and dislikes. To me, they suck every goodness out of the ground. They don't belong.

I'm ranting!

Who for?

Just me.

I paused at the arched gateway into the churchyard on account of the memories I have of that spot.

I took a moment to sit on the mounting block just by the gateway. We'd sit there and talk when we were young.

Anyway, I walked through into the churchyard, passing the church on my way to the lychgate. I didn't go in. From the lychgate, I looked out over the marketplace with its rows of stalls around the Moot Hall.

As far as I know the magistrate's court and council chamber are still in the Moot Hall.

It's years since I was last there.

I can see The Shambles on the other side of the marketplace. Mr Linn had the Gem Shop in The Shambles. I know Tom lives in the flat above the shop. I had the impulse to calling to see if he was in. I pushed it aside. It's been too long.

I still have the little lodestone Mr Linn gave me when Austin died. He gave one to Tom and me, telling us to hold onto it if we felt unsure which way to turn in life. I've had mine hanging from my keyring ever since.

I doubled back from the lychgate and had a wander round the church.

The font is just inside the door. I know it was installed by the vicar after Lilburne's siege. It has an inscription in latin every child at St John's learned by heart, 'Baptisterium bello Phanaticorum dirutum, de nuovo erectum'. It means something like, 'installed after the time of the fanatics'. It makes perfect sense to me.

I'd forgotten about the lancet windows at the east end. Sunlight streamed through, splashing colour over the sanctuary floor and into the choir stalls. Some caught the edge of the tomb of Richard de Elstern. I remember learning about him. He was a crusader knight: captured, ransomed and returned home.

The tomb says he died at home of 'the flux'.

That's the shits.

Imagine that!

Tragic and pointless.

I sat in the choir stalls where I did as a boy.

We wore blue cassocks and had ruffs round our necks back then.

I don't suppose they have a choir now.

The Vicar's stall is next to where I'm sitting. Opposite is where old Father Robert sat. He was Master when I was young. He had blue lips and man boobs. As boys, we sniggered at his old man tits.

The thing I remember most about Father Robert was his kindness.

What a thing to be remembered for, being kind. Wouldn't that be perfect?

Pearl told me once that my obituary should be 'He thought too much.' I'd take 'He was kind' any day.

Father Robert wore a white poppy every Remembrance Sunday. He'd stand next to dad at the cenotaph. They wore their medals and dad wore his regimental tie.

I can picture Mr Ormerod and Peado Ronnie in the back row across the chancel from where I'm sitting.

Mr Ormerod used to glare at Simon. As he sang, his poppy-out eyes would reach across the chancel, inspecting our every gesture.

Peado Ronnie never looked directly at us. He'd give a sideways lear and the slightest smear of a slimy smirk.

Dad said Peado Ronnie was too 'free'. He didn't like me near him.

I found where I scratched my initials in the pew and ran my finger along the mark. It was naughty of me to scratch my name. I'm guilty of that little bit of unseen graffiti.

It's nice remember those days in the choir, even making some graffiti.

I can see the church from where I'm sitting at my table in the cafe window. It sits in its neat, clipped picture postcard churchyard, weathered gravestones and all.

I wonder what people see when they look across to this elegant Georgian terrace.

In a way this terrace is graffiti.

Its centrepiece is the church of St Charles Borromeo.

I learned about when I went to Milan Cathedral. He was a Medici. Archbishop of Milan. He oppressed protestants or did he just assert the Roman church? I suppose it depends where you stand.

I wonder if the people of St John's would have thought about that when the earl and his French countess, built this terrace on the footprint of buildings smashed by the Protestant, Calvinist, Puritan, Baptist Lilburne?

It's troubling to think this terrace is not that different to my graffiti on a choir stall.

My mind has wandered to a catholic priest I read about in Pontefract. Henry Hammerton, he tried to set up a chapel and school. The people rioted and he was driven out of town. It was only in the 1860s. Not that long ago really.

Steve told me his family name is Huguenot. His family fled France because of catholic oppression. They settled in Yorkshire. His name is like graffiti. He can't rub it out. It's like a tattoo, a permanent mark of who he is.

I suppose my name isn't much different. Ayton. We've always been in Elsternwick and Bran, there's always been a Bran Ayton.

We can't ignore the graffiti.

The Moot Hall in the marketplace is part of Elsternwick's graffiti.

It's a digression but I feel I need to write that I hate it when people refer to a 'mute point' instead of 'moot point'.

Mute is silent. It says nothing.

Moot says all that might be said.

People came here with the earl to listen to everything that might be said and to make judgements.

I wonder what they all said about the terrace in North Bar and the church of St Charles Borromeo?

The Moot Hall is where the wapentake of Elstern met, as they called it.

I like that word, *wapentake*. It comes from *weapon shake*. The people came to make their decisions about the life in the marketplace.

I like it.

Anyway. I love the ordinariness and the chatter and bustle of markets.

The cheese seller from Saxby market has a stall here too. I don't think she saw me.

I climbed the steps to the Moot Hall. You can see across the marketplace towards St John's from there. It's where the earl and High Steward pronounced judgement.

The gallows would have been in front of the Moot Hall steps.

They're a chilling thought. I guess there has to be judgement. You can't just stay in the marketplace and wander round aimlessly. You can't just stay, pretending to be holy. There has to be judgement.

I suppose balanced judgement comes through listening.

The thought leads me back to the motto in the plaster freeze on the cafe wall:
    Viam prudentiae ostendit - Prudence Shows the Way.

I'm forced to think about this business of prudence, the wisdom that knows the way through wastelands and marketplaces where truth is found.

Day 22

I used to love coming up to these ruined castle walls. They were torn down by Lilburne after the siege. They're high on the crag above Elsternwick. Looking down from here gives fresh perspective on Elsternwick's isolation. I can look down into Dell Woods clinging to the hillside below the castle, wrapping dark skirts between the crag and the town

Beyond the woods, I can see St John's and the Georgian terrace with the church of St Charles Borromeo with its cupola centrepiece, hidden from the street by the terrace pediment. Looking down from here, all I have in my mind are fanatics hurling wordless petards across the street.

I can remember a cartoon Father Robert gave me as a boy when I was in the choir at St John's. He'd cut it out of the paper and stuck it on a bigger paper so I wouldn't lose it. I had it on my wall for years. In the cartoon a girl says to a boy, 'I was a good evangelist at school' The boy then ask's 'How'd you do that' and she replied, 'I hit some kid with my lunch box'.

It's all they did: hit one another with lunch boxes.

Is that all these pitiful divisions are, nothing but factious, peevish fanatics hitting each other with their lunch boxes and missing the point.

Weak and feeble fanatics!

What an irony: power craving fanatics are just the weak and feeble.

It makes me wonder what the opposite might be. Strong and courageous, I suppose.

I wonder what the strong and courageous do?

Which am I most like?

An easy answer is tempting!

Turning round I can see across the expanse of grass, the Stryd.

It's one of those words of Elsternwick, Stryd. It means 'street'. It's from the old days.

When I was young, the Stryd as a place to play. Now I see it with different eyes.

Centuries ago, people lived and worked here, inside the castle's curtain wall. There are raised flat mounds in two rows either side of a long, wide pathway. Near the centre is the Temple.

It's not a real temple. The earl built it when he came back from his Grand Tour.

It confuses me. He built the church of St Charles Borromeo and the Temple. Surely you should be one thing or another?

The earl cleared away the ruined Keep, smashed by Lilburne. He built the Manor and his own greek temple.

I think I'll walk over and write from the Temple for a bit.

There are four steps up from ground level to what remains of the mosaic floor. What was it they called those little bits they made mosaics from? I think they're called tesserae. Yes I'm sure that's right. There're pretty-well gone now.

I'm writing with my back to one of the columns and looking towards the ruin of the curtain wall. Pearl sat in this spot in the photograph in my memory box.

I can picture her, a little waif; scrawny in skinny jeans and a cowl-neck top, a tumble of ash blond hair tied back in a loose ponytail.

Away to my right are the ruins of the High Gate barbican. I can hear the Ravens rasping *'caw'*. I don't know why Lilburne didn't tear the whole thing down.

I'm enjoying just sitting.

I had such happy times here.

It's just that I wanted more.

I think you do when you are young.

I wonder what I thought 'more' was.

I wonder what 'more' is.

I wonder what 'enough' is? - I remember someone very wise telling me, 'you have to know what enough is'.

I doubt I've ever known.

Why is that?

It's starting to rain. I don't think it'll be too bad.

I'm going to have a wander through Dell Woods. It'll be sheltered under the trees.

INTERLUDE WHILST I TAKE A WALK IN DELL WOODS

I've driven down from the top of Sally Lane and I'm writing on the bench where I sat with Pearl last year. It's become an important place to me.

Earlier this morning, I'd parked across from Dell Cottage, just below the old Sally Port. That's where Lilburne first breached the Curtain Wall.

I rushed back to the car when it started to rain, so I didn't get soaked. I waited there until it bated.

You don't hear 'bated' used much. I don't know why. It's popped into my mind just now. We think of 'bated breath' for that sort of holding your breath in suspense. I wonder why we describe rain specifically as having 'bated'. I know it means 'stopping' or 'being held off'. I suppose we describe someone's anger being 'abated', although that feels even more archaic. It's just funny how we apply the word to rain stopping but I can't think of other times we use it. Maybe it's just me. I don't know.

Anyway, the word caught my attention.

I've just thought of another word: 'laik'.

Mr Johnson came round to mend the roof the other week. I was having a day off and he described me as 'laikin'. I'd not heard the word for years.

The kids in the Burgages used it when I was young. I wasn't allowed to use it. Mum said it wasn't good English. I had to say 'playing'.

The sound of the rain dripping onto the car's roof was hypnotic. I rolled down the window to stop the car from steaming up completely. The damp air was full of the smell of fresh spring rain on wet ground and of garlic from the woods.

Lovely.

I got out of the car when the rain finally stopped and took the path into the Dell, sunlight streaming through the trees. Shafts of light picked up bright sweeps of bluebells.

I took the path off to the right and picked my way through the trailing, brambles to find the large flat stone that sits above the Dell. From this stone, the ground falls away over a little gritstone crag of no more than three or four metres. It was clear of brambles years ago. Now it's overgrown. When I was a boy there was an almost perfect semi-circle around the foot of the crag, a little amphitheatre.

I remember four faces, laid out in tesserae below the crag: Air, Earth Water and Fire. Like the Temple on the Stryd, they'd been put there by the earl. I don't know why. I couldn't see them as I looked from the stone. I expect they've been overgrown.

The stone was a place we shared dreams and hopes when we were young.

We used to lie back and look up to the dappling light through the high branches of Ash and Birch. I was worried someone might come by and see me lounging around, perhaps thinking I'm up to no good.

For goodness sake what, 'up to no good' could there have been?

Why couldn't I just lie back to enjoy and remember.

Even though it felt silly, I did it.

Closing my eyes and concentrating, I heard my friends chattering and wondering; dreaming about life and the future of what might be.

I didn't want to sit up. More than that, I felt tied down there. Held by all those dreams and memories.

The light through the trees, the smell of the damp woods, the wind gently moving the leaves; they were intoxicating. I drifted off and was brought round by the sound of children playing beyond the Dell. It sparked a memory of something that happened here.

I'd come up to the stone but heard voices and the crack of an airgun.

It's as if I can hear them now.

Back then, I was stupid.

I sneaked across the Dell to take a look.

It turned out to be Simon and Nobby firing an airgun at a coke can on a tree stump.

The other voices belonged to Jem and Pearl.

I watched Nobby strip a reed and blow down it. He chewed paper to make a pellet, firing it at Jem. I saw her duck. It missed her and she laughed.

He darted to the right, diving to the ground and catching a frog. Holding tight, he pushed the reed in the frog's mouth and blew hard. I knew it would swell to burst.

I remember being angry and ridiculously principled. I cried out and fell, sliding down the muddy bank.

Simon grabbed me, pulling my shirt.

Jem and Pearl were silent.

Something made me fight back.

Simon and Nobby pushed me into the mud at the edge of the pond.

I was covered in cold, wet mud. I can feel it squelching through my fingers even now.

I couldn't get away.

They came towards me. Staying out of the mud, they threw stones to splash me.

I was trapped.

I knew I'd have to see Simon in church on Sunday. He would be saintly-nice to me.

I'd be trapped there too.

I watched Pearl and Jem sneak behind Nobby and Simon, fingers to their lips motioning me to keep quiet.

The stones still hit me and splashed mud over me.

All in a moment the girls pushed.

Down the boys went; into the mud with me.

I scrambled up and was away running faster than them.

I left the shouting behind along with the girls laughter.

Lying back on the stone, eyes shut but aware of the light, I wondered who was humbled more; me or Simon and Nobby?

Sitting here now, I wonder about the way those experiences have formed the 'me' I am.

I think Simon and Nobby saw me as quiet and a bit stuck up.

I never wanted to play to that image, like some puppet dangling from other people's strings.

I've spent I my whole life risking falling down slippery banks, turning fear of it into excitement.

Simon and Nobby's bullying wasn't about hurting me. It was just showing off. I happened to be there. They were wrong and cruel. In the end they were in the same mess as me. We were no different.

Sitting here on this bench, I'm thinking about how I was caught up in something over which I had little control. I'd just allowed myself to go there.

Anyway I'd better end this and get back to Tess's. I'm looking forward to the pub tonight.

Day 23

Tess knocked at the door. She left coffee and buttered toast just outside the bedroom door.

She's gone to open up the bookshop she manages downstairs.

Last night was an experience not to be missed!

I've a banging headache.

I'm sitting on the edge of my bed writing this.

So much happened last night. I need to try and capture it all. Even with my hangover, I feel I learned more about myself last night than during the whole of my time writing in my Cupola room. More importantly, I enjoyed myself.

How would I sum up last night? Surreal in its ridiculousness and humbling in its effect. That's a characteristically arsy sentence. I'm sticking with it. Those adjectives work: surreal, ridiculous, humbling.

I was taken back in time. They saw the lad I was, the lad I am.

Fool that I am, I was so desperate to project the man I've become.

The only parallel I can draw is when you stand on the edge of a swimming pool. You know the water will be really cold compared to where you are on the edge. You know you'll be OK when you get in and it's always better to jump in. In spite of that, you get in bit by bit.

Last night I was pushed in.

I'd been spotted by Donna.

Beer bottle in hand, she flung herself at me screeching a terrifying, 'Bran Ayton. It's Bran Ayton!' - She saw me as soon as I opened the door.

Before I knew it, arms were round me and beer spilled down my back from the bottle loosely attached to her hand. A kiss found itself planted on my lips with over decorated lips.

I couldn't peel her off. I'm not sure about the moist sensation round my mouth even now.

I had to prise her off, unwinding her from round my neck.

Donna was a sight to behold, with red spiked hair and Widow Twanky frock of petrol blue with its cerise pink flower motif. Evidently she was waiting for her 'partner'. She emphasised the first three letters of the word 'PARtner' with an alarming punch that matched the vigour of her embrace.

I'd tried to back away but failed.

Having pacified me, she explained intricate details of her life. Words flowed from her like water from a broken pipe, spilling out in a gushing flood.

We plumbed the depths as she gave an account of her oral hygiene, demonstrated in the removal of her teeth. She held her dentures towards me, spittle dripping between thumb and forefinger. Her lips collapsed in on her mouth and she described the challenges of meeting her PARtner's demands for a blowjob without teeth, creating a mass of spittle. Evidently this was an unacceptably over-lubricated experience.

To my horror now, I half remember limply suggesting she swallow harder. Pinned down by her, I suppose I wanted to be helpful.

Her PARtner appeared. The horrific Neville.

In the moment, I'd forgotten about him.

Without a word he pulled her away. I responded, raising my hands in involuntary apology. That would be of no use to Neville.

I heard laughter behind me and turned to look. I saw Martin first. I don't know why he and I lost contact? I suppose it's just life.

I know Martin married 'Miss Deb's', as Carolyn calls her, but still lives his dream playing at gigs in the Queens. I'm sure they make a perfect couple. I'm not surprised she wasn't there last night.

I heard he went out with Pearl after she and I broke up.

He came over and hugged me like a brother I can't deny I was embarrassed. (Hugging isn't what I do). He took me over to the table where everyone from years and years ago was chatting.

There was no jockeying for position, no competitiveness, no reaching for this or that. They just were as they always have been. It felt good.

I was a bit unnerved when Simon and Nobby joined us. Simon struggled to walk across the room and needed Nobby's help. His right arm was limp and useless. He looked gaunt. His long tousle of back hair had become thin and grey. I felt unsure, remembering his reputation.

Nobby was imposing, with those piercing eyes. Full sleeves of tattoos covered taught biceps and climbed round his neck. He sat the other side of Simon helping him with his drink, steading him on his seat.

Jem whispered that they live together behind the Spice Market. Evidently they've both come out and are in a Civil Partnership.

Nobby called Simon, 'Spacka'. I was shocked.

Why would Nobby use such a horrible name? I couldn't quite square the circle that makes it right to call anyone 'Spacka', still less someone you care for.

Then again I remember thinking about Mr Hetherington the other day and how grandma called him 'cripple' and 'lame'.

I suppose words bubble up in the middle of life. I don't suppose it's possible to legislate for language. I know the politically correct brigade try.

It's a bit of digression but I'm reminded of that woman who referred to her own children as 'half-cast'. She told me once that some social worker berated her and she told her, 'They're my girls and I'll call them 'half cast' if I want, because it's what they are.'

Why should bland supremacists bleach language to suit themselves?

I like that term, 'bland supremacist'. It just popped into my head. I think I'll write it as a noun, Bland Supremacist, alongside White Supremacist and Black Supremacist.

Anyway, back to last night.

Neville appeared one last time. The band played some 1970s Punk. When they got to the Strangler's and No More Heroes. Neville burst onto the dance floor, pot belly bouncing along as he tried to relive 1977.

He failed.

I doubt he knows who Leon Trotsky or Lenin were, still less Elmyra or Sancho Panza. Then again I wonder if asking that question makes me more of a moron than Neville.

I don't actually know who Elmyra was, except the cartoon character. I wonder if anyone knows?

As to Sancho Panza, at least he followed Don Quixote, trying to be chivalrous, even if he ended up pointlessly tilting at windmills.[18]. Sancho Panaza gave up ideas of power and influence going back to being a servant as I recall. I like that.

Anyway, that's an arsy digression.

I think all Neville wanted was to remember the Strangers and 1977.

When we were young, all he wanted was to be noticed. He had fat, rosy-red cheeks not unlike my image of Sancho Panza I suppose. He had acne and would scratch and pick, making scars. We were cruel to him. I was cruel, to my shame. Boastful and braggy, he'd push himself forward, imposing his opinion.

He was distasteful.

He's still short.

He wanted to join the police or the army or something. He was too short.

To my cost, he's a Traffic Warden.

Last night in the Gig room with his Sex Pistol's t-shirt and spiked hair Neville was a mass of frustration.

I was watching him and Jem leaned across and whispered, 'you know they call him Thrush?' Simon heard and smirked saying, 'He's a scratchy cunt'.

Mid-song there was turmoil.

I caught sight of Neville falling backwards in my direction. Over to my left, Nobby moved with such speed. Chairs flew like chaff. He was between Neville and the big younger lad who'd pushed him to the floor. He thought better of a confrontation with Nobby in full force.

In one movement Nobby went from his chair to defending Neville, to helping him up. All of this before the rest of us reacted.

To my shame, I was frozen to the spot.

---

[18] M de Cervantes. Don Quixote, (1605) translated by E Grossman, Harper Collins (2003)

Bemused, I shuffled closer to Simon making room for Neville and Donna.

I'd love to be able to write something with an air of superiority about Neville reflecting my personal high ground. I can't. I feel for him in what I see to be his embarrassment. More than that. I'm with him in it, although I hate that thought.

I envy Nobby his quick actions and morality, although to anyone outside the situation, he'd be seen as an aggressor.

I think I'm upright and moral. I wonder who those old friends see? They don't see my standing or reputation. They see me. That's how it should be. I know it is.

I sometimes say to Pearl that I see the woman she is and the girl she was. I think that's what acceptance is about. These old friends are the same. That's why I found myself with them. It's why they widened their group to make room for Neville and Donna.

There was Neville on the dance floor: fat, peevish and factious, taking a moment to live a harmless dream.

It seems to me, that's OK. - Life goes on around him. Nothing much changes.

Martin's no different. He's living his dream, playing his gigs. I just happen to like him.

I guess Martin's dream may extend to Pearl. I know they've been to other gigs together and haven't told Debs. Pearl wouldn't be interested in more than the company dismissing Debs as 'his shit'. I'm not so sure about Martin and his secret world.

What about Simon and Nobby? They live their dream. Their reality is caring for each other. I'm not sure it's that obvious.

Day 24

I've parked the car here at the Look Out.

I've had such a good time back home in Elsternwick.

What a strange thing, I used the phrase 'back home'. I've not thought of Elsternwick as home for half a lifetime. That's how it feels right now: home.

If it wasn't for lovely Tess, I'd never have gone.

I'm struck by how I'm caught up in her warmth. It wasn't that different last night.

Old friends just saw 'me'; no pressure, no posturing, no pretence. More to the point, there was no running and hiding. There's just being acceptance, feeling I'm known.

Now I'm on my way back home.

Now that's interesting. I'm going home, to my house in Saxby but I've called Elsternwick home too. I can't help thinking of Elsternwick as home. Over all these years, I've tried not to be from there. The thing is, it's where I'm from. No. It's more than that. Deep down, it's where I belong.

Anyway, for now, I'm parked at the Look Out, half way between Elsternwick and Pullen Bridge. This is such a stark place, jutting out of the marshy ings and the expanse of sands. A little noticeboard says the marshes and sands are an 'area of special scientific interest' and that they're dangerous, so not to stray onto them.

The tide is beginning to come in. Fingers of water are stretching across the sands. I wouldn't like to be out there. I'm watching two or three shadows of people out there in the distance. Rather them than me.

When I was young, we learned about Secret Ways across the sands and warned never to walk them alone.

The people out there must know what they're doing with the tide coming in.

It's flooding the low sand beds, making what looks like ridges stand out.

I wouldn't like to be caught out there.

I've heard stories of smugglers out on those Secret Ways and of course Lilburne's vanguard led to their ruin. Who knows the truth in any of them. They're children's stories. Myths.

Looking back towards Elsternwick, the inscription on the bridge is in my mind. '*Weep not for the past. Fear not for the future*'. I can't say I've ever wept for the past.

I like the phrase, '*fear not for the future*'. I love the idea of turning fear into excitement about what could happen.

I've just glanced over to where I saw the people on the sands. They've disappeared.

My mind has flit back to Pearl. I can't say why. One thought leads to another with no obvious connection, I suppose.

I'm thinking about her nickname, Pearl. I don't know why I've never called her by her name, Margaret, Margaret Fleet.

Everyone calls her Maggie. I call her Pearl.

It's because of that single black teardrop pearl she wears. She's always worn it, so far as I can remember. I've never asked her about it. It's a strange thing.

I know they used to harvest pearls from oyster beds in the estuary. They've gone now. Fished out and died out I think. Such a shame.

I suppose I must be tired after my weekend. My mind is wandering around random connections: Elsternwick, the Secret Ways, pearls.

Every now and then I was young, we'd go for Sunday tea at Elstern Manor. There was a painting hanging in the West Range, a Holbein I think. It was of the earl with Thomas Wriothesley, Earl of Southampton. If I remember, he was Henry VIII's henchman. They're pouring over papers, surrounded by boxes of treasure. I remember the painting's title, A Letter of Marque. It's funny what comes to mind.

It would be a bit fanciful to anyone else; I wonder if Pearl's family were caught up in all of that.

She and I are of this place, of Elsternwick. It's in our bones.

Anyway, I ought to get back. I can't sit here all day, much as I'd like to.

I'm ending this with my thoughts dwelling on the people out on the sands. I can't imagine where they've got to. Maybe I imagined them? Who knows?

Perhaps I really am over-thinking.

Day 25

I slept soundly last night and woke with words from one of the songs on the CD rattling round in my head.

'I'll catch you when you fall'.[19] I've never felt anyone would catch me.

I'm writing this on the terrace looking over the estuary. I'm drinking coffee and reflecting on the last few days.

I feel comfortable and at peace. For all the quietness in my heart, I believe I've misunderstood so much.

I've built my security in this house. I can come in and lock the door behind me and feel safe. From my Cupola room, I can look over the estuary and see Elsternwick and be reminded.

Yet there's a restless deep inside.

It feels as if I've been walking blindfold. At least that was my dream last night.

I dreamed I was walking on the Secret Ways and at the same time standing on the Look Out watching a shadowy me on the sands.

As I watched, I knew I had to trust I'd follow the right path.

A cold wind whipped around me as, in my dream I watched from the Look Out. There was a single word on the wind. It hissed: 'Redemption', 'Redemption', 'Redemption'......on and on and on.

It chided and goaded me.

Somehow, I knew I must prepare to pay the cost, but what cost and whatever for, I'm not sure. In my dream I knew I couldn't stay on the Look Out, I had to step onto the sands.

The thing is, I don't mind stepping out.

I want to pay.

If I can have this feeling of peace, this quiet, I'll sell all I have for it and do all I need to do.

---

[19] S Earle, When I Fall (2000) Songwriter, S Earle, Label E-Squared

Who wouldn't do the same, giving all they have to be redeemed like this, to have this peace, this quiet?

In fact today I was so elated with the joy of knowing what I need to do, I acted out of character.

It's something I haven't done it since I was a boy.

I felt stupid but loved it.

No-one was around.

I let rip.

Why shouldn't I?

I did what I call, the 'stick thing'.

I did it when I was a boy.

I used my walking stick, the one Doris gave me.

It's hawthorn.

Doris said Hawthorn was for protection, that it was the wood Jesus' crown of thorns was made from.

Why that would matter to her, I'm not sure.

Anyway, Hawthorn walking stick is part of who I am. I like it.

Doris was a strange old bird. I suppose she had a lot to put up with in Peado Ronnie.

There were stories about him.

There's probably a lot in them.

He jiggled my balls once.

I remember his hand reaching down.

I felt the grip.

Perv.

I stopped going round.

I never told dad or mum. Dad never liked me going. I don't know why I went.

Why did that memory surface?

I've not thought of Doris and Ronnie for years. Was something darker going on? I suppose it's best to leave it be.

I imagine the people around me in the street as I walk to work with my fedora and my walking stick. I don't mind being a cartoon, a flickering image of my Self. They don't know the real 'me'.

Oh God, did Ronnie 'hide' behind Doris? Oh fuck!

I'm going to dark places.

I'd rather write about the stick thing.

It was a happy, simple thing.

I ran the stick along the railings today as I went home along Hobbe Syke. It felts a silly, childish thing to do. I loved the sound: *clack, clack, clack* and the happiness it gave me.

No-one saw.

I was a boy again.

It reminded me of running up Sally Lane to the Dell, clattering sticks along the railings over the bridge where the beck rushes down Warden's Gylle.

Today, I was that boy again with my *clack, clack clack* in the railings. I loved it.

I have the façade of the man they expect; a cartoon character of establishment order.

I'd rather be clattering my stick along the railings.

Inside, beneath the cartoon I'm just a boy.

I need to let the boy out; clattering my stick.

This is about me, the boy, the person I am: Bran.

Day 26

I've been to the Ring O' Bells. It's late but despite the time, I want to write.

So much is going on in my head.

I need to get it all down. I'm writing in the kitchen with red wine and a fried egg sandwich. I shouldn't. Who cares.

I went to the 'Saxby on the Move' neighbourhood meeting tonight. It was against my better judgement.

I felt I ought to show my face.

I rewarded myself by going to the Ring O' Bells for the last hour. I'd heard they had Hambleton brewery's Nightmare, their Yorkshire Porter as guest beer. I love it!

I had one too many, so might have misunderstood the bizarre conversation I had with the new barmaid. Sitting here, I remember it as more a series of strange digressions I couldn't fathom than a conversation. We jumped from one to another, like stepping stones across a river.

She told me she believed vegan werwolves exist. Evidently she'd been convinced by someone she trusted.

I worked out the source of her conviction through the next stepping stone digression.

She fired a question at me while pulling my pint, 'Do you believe in Zombie's too?'

The word 'too' was a clue, helped by a nod over my left shoulder and her telling me it was, 'them two' who'd convinced her.

There were alternatives, Chris and Steve sitting by the window or the Derricks at the other end of the bar. They're not known for either humour or imagination.

I think it's just me who calls them the Derricks. It's my humour, my coming to terms with them. They're a pair of nasty, cruel bastards. They're both called Derick and schizophrenic reputations, for being everso worthy, whilst quietly and insidiously strangling and twisting anything that doesn't fit their view of the world. They make me so angry. I call them Sanctimonious and Humpty-back and change the spelling to Derrick because they seem hang their victims out to dry. I have a cartoon in my head of them binding good people and hanging them to be pilloried

107

Bastards.

Anyway, back to the zombie story.

It had to be Chris and Steve.

Evidently they'd talked about the 'strange recluse' in the house in Hobbe Wood and how they thought he might be a zombie.

She blinked staring eyes at me through gold-rimmed glasses and then looked away, letting me drop like a stone. She looked back and picked me up again.

It was very disconcerting, since I'm the 'strange recluse', although definitely not a zombie.

Before she brought me my pint, I'd been watching her singing and dancing away to Spandau Ballet at the other end of the bar. She was in her own little world.

Tiny with pink and blue hair tied into plaits that bounced around as she danced, she had piercing eyes behind those round, gold-rimmed glasses. Her eyes blinked big, slow, interested blinks. She was pretty and not pretty at the same time. I couldn't age her. I sensed she wasn't in her twenties. She could have been in her fifties. She was strange one.

The pint she pulled came with more unconnected questions.

With direct and inappropriate impertinence she asked what was in my satchel.

Before I could answer, she explained she was convinced vegan werwolves wouldn't hurt people, would eat just 'veg-ta-bles' and were probably buddhist.

I wanted to ask if she was on drugs.

I didn't.

I guessed she was.

Then we were back onto the zombie in Hobbe Wood.

I know I stood blinking at her, speechless. She blinked back.

She held me with her blinks and asked my name.

I told her.

Swinging her left bosom at me across the bar she told me her's was Eli.

The bosom swinging wasn't improper. Her name badge had hung there but had been lost. I assume she thought it was still there.

She went on almost laughing, 'Bran?! Isn't that a breakfast cereal to make you go'?......and...... 'What were your parents thinking of'.

I spluttered beer over the bar trying to hold back laughter and asked if Eli was short for Eleanor.

She said, it's just Eli and spelled it out 'E'-'L'-'I', telling me people often think it's spelled 'E'-'L'-'L'-'I'-'E'.

Her eyes flared emphasis through those gold-rimmed glasses as she said, 'I am who I am, simply Eli'.

She told me a bit of her story, which had been about rootless drifting from moment to moment, experience to experience, living whatever came along.

Randomly, she ask again what was in my satchel.

This time I showed her.

She ignored Pearl's scarf, grabbing my journal and flicked through it. It felt like an invasion.

She tossed it back in my satchel with a simple:
> 'Me and the universe get on with whatever comes our way. We don't think much, me and the universe. '

I admire people who trust the flow of life, but she believes in vegan werwolves!

I have to admit, I left the bar happier for the conversation and went to sit with Steve and Chris. They greeted me like two howling wolves.

I didn't mind.

Eli threw thinking into neutral. Nothing had meaning, except in the moment. For me, she's naive and gullible. For her everything that's true is now, in the moment.

As I sit here dribbling egg yoke from my sandwich, I suspect she sees more than me.

So what about the 'Saxby On The Move' neighbourhood group tonight?

It was a *ra-ra-ra* community meeting. Not really my thing but I joined conversation about street cleaning, dog shit and groups of young people hanging about on street corners.

The meeting was full of the expected collection of the bossy and the nosey and the willing. Some had hobbyhorses, some go to everything. Two made me smile. One was very vocal and procedural. He was keen on points of order in that polite but firm way. The other had the English accent of cut glass, strawberry tea at the tennis club and the BBC. She had an air of entitlement that is the preserve of the English middle classes.

Cut Glass said, 'one' a lot.

Saying 'one' irritates me, when what is meant is 'I'.

They say, 'One thinks that' and 'One does that'. They mean 'I think that' and 'I do that' or 'I thought that' or 'I did that'; not fucking 'One thought' or 'One did'.

I get so cross. Anyway, it seems to be just a particular category of the stuck up middle classes who do it. I just get irritated, that's all.

Enough of that. If Cut Glass said 'one' a lot, the other one, didn't say it at all. He said, 'I', 'me', 'my' and 'our'.

Anyway, they'd each lost a front tooth.

Polite and opinionated in different way's they'd each lost a tooth but hadn't rushed to the dentist.

I'd hate not to have a front tooth.

I wonder what it is that makes me laugh when people don't fit my expectations?

I wouldn't be surprised to see tooth gaps on a sink estate, but not here. What is it that drives this?

I wonder what the toothless ones see in themselves?

Do they notice their dental deficit?

I doubt they consider it for even a moment.

It's interesting to thinking about what drives the judgements we make.

I wonder, would the toothless poor think more or less about their lack of dentures compared to the toothless middle-classes? It seems a pointless question, but it's loaded with layers of other questions that fascinate me.

Cut Glass, is an allotment holding environmentalist. For some reason beyond my understanding, she held forth about Aristoxenus. I've heard of him.

She reminds me of the man who called round to try and sell me a hot tub for the terrace. He had a spherical body, a red face and was from Barnsley and keen to tell me he had a masters degree in Cognitive Psychology. Why shouldn't he!

He held forth about human collective consciousness. He didn't just say, 'I', 'me', 'you, 'we' and 'our' but adds, 'thee' and thar' and never ever says 'one', except as a number.

I can remember one of the things he said. It ran something like this:
'R thinks all't time tha nos but tha knows ow it is r' cunt stop thinkin' 'bart it, till a'd thowert on and thowert on it again. Sum tiams, durst tha not think wi' think t' much but just carn't stop it cos it's just ow we'r' wired?'

I liked him. He threw me a bit, lecturing me on the finer points of Cognitive Psychology, but it seems to me he's right.

Pearl is always saying I think too much, but here we have this hot tub seller telling me we humans just can't help ourselves. It's not an act of the will we have much choice about.

I was reminded of the hot tub salesman by something Cut Glass said. She told the whole meeting about Aristoxenus' difficulty with Pythagoras.

Wonderful!

I'm not sure an obscure Greek philosopher would normally show up in a polite neighbourhood meeting. She told us about Artisonexus' emphasis was on harmony and that he argued with Pythagoras who liked rules.

I prefer rules. I'm comfortable with Pythagorus.

Her point was that Aristoxenus' concern was with the way people encountered music, not the music's structure. At least that sounded to be the heart of the issue.

For Cut Glass, what matters most is the quality of people's relationships rather than the rules by which they live?

Perhaps she's right; perhaps Eli is.

111

Day 27

Too much good beer and a late night writing my journal didn't put me in a good place this morning! Thankfully today, wasn't too taxing.

I thought I'd take time trying to relax and take a different tack today. Aside from still not feeling quite myself, I had an intriguing meeting today that's made me think.

I met Dolores.

We'd not met before.

I've no idea why but she poured her heart out.

Apparently, she feels herself an imposter.

Dolores the Imposter. Those words combine nicely when I say them out loud. I mean the sound of them combines nicely, not the meaning.

We met for coffee at the station cafe. She was sitting in a saggy armchair when I arrived. It almost had a life of its own, having wrapped itself round her and sucked her in.

Dolores was very small and reminded me of a shrew.

She drank coffee with quick little sips, while gulped by the armchair.

Her hair was dyed and not well cut. It flopped about, part covering her face.

She wore austere rectangular, horn-rimmed glasses that were the wrong shape for her long face.

Her lips were smeared bright red. Smeared is a more appropriate word than applied. Lipstick spilled over the margins of her ample lips.

I saw myself reflected in her intensity.

She inspected me.

I was a fly on a pin.

She explained herself, making her confession.

It was my confession.

She's no imposter, even though she felt so.

She feels she'll be found out, so she works harder to prove herself.

It was a bit random. She told me about her horse.

Apparently she's new to horses owning.

I tried to picture this tiny, woman with smear-red lips marshalling some great stallion. The picture made me want to smile to the point of laughter. I had to stop myself by concentrating on something else. It was an act of the will.

Cartoon images of huge horses and tiny riders kept floating through my mind, making me smile.

I tried concentrate on her nose. I fixed my gaze on it. Mesmerised by its slight movement up and down ever as she took bites from a cinnamon bun.

I suppose it was something to do with the shape of her head and those teeth but, as I think about it now I can't get a cartoon image of a horse ravaging a cinnamon bun out of my mind.

Is ravaging the right word, with its connotation of passion? I suppose I mean more, obliteration, wrecking destruction by those teeth.

Ravaging will do for the cartoon in my head. I'm not sure it will do for Dolores. She seemed too small to ravage anything, even a cinnamon bun. Appearances can be deceptive I suppose.

I confess, I don't feel I have control over these cartoons.

It has to be admitted, Dolores' teeth were a curiosity. They seemed to be trying to escape her mouth in different directions all at once.

Anyway our conversation bored me, but Dolores fascinated me.

In normal business-like conversation we prioritise detail. In my conversation with Dolores, incidental stories of horses and teeth and smeared lipstick were my priority, diverting me from her obsession with proving herself.

I found myself thinking, 'why on earth can't you just enjoy yourself.' The setting wouldn't allow the thought to mature into words. Anyway, it made me look a little too hard at my own reflection.

114

Now I feel I an imposter. My mind wasn't where it should've been. I'm not sure it's where it should be now, although I'm wondering if I know where 'should' might 'be'.

As to Dolores, I did try to gather my thoughts, liberally dispensing affirming nods across the sea of coffee in my own cup.

I looked across at her and through my own horn-rimmed glasses.

Who am I to reflect on Dolores?

Am I more or less an imposter than her?

Who would know?

Anyway, Dolores feels herself an imposter.

I know how she feels.

It sometimes feels as if I shouldn't be here, with all this.

It turns out she justifies herself by what she achieves and how she's seen.

As for me, the more I achieve, the more I feel I'm heaping up a dung heap of nothing.

Who am I to mentor Dolores?

That's what she wanted. She thought I'd be able to give her some direction.

I wish I thought that might be possible, or rather worthwhile.

I'm happy to give it a go but I'm not confident I have much to offer, except coat tails to hang on to.

Day 28

I've been to another head-up-your-arse evening at the Old Court House. It was all about 'What Contributes to Well-Being in Society' and was part of Saxby-on-the-Move week.

They'd wheeled in three speakers from the House of Lords and lined up retired professor of Theoretical Physics, Bob Burley-Browne to chair proceedings. He seemed an odd choice. Actually he made my head explode. He said he wanted to give us a new way of seeing based on what he called, non-Euclidian geometry. I wondered what the fuck he was on, but he turned out to be quite good

I want to try and make sense of what he was talking about.

He had us imagine an orbit round the earth, through the north and the south poles. We had to imagine flying round time and time again. He said, we could fly round the earth infinitely but each orbit was finite. I get that, the infinite (endless flying) in the finite (the limits of the circle).

Then he had us, imagine two of these orbits, which he called 'great circles', each going through the north and south poles and then a third that was horizontal around the earth. Then he had us think about the horizontal line joining two vertical lines to create a triangle. Finally, he asked us how many angles it took to form that triangle. People shouted out, '180°'. I was among them.

He mocked.

He called us 'Flatlanders'[20] telling us the actual total of the angles of a triangle on a sphere is slightly more than 180° and called this difference, 'spherical excess'.

He explained, we'd learned our rules from Pythagorus when we were at school, but those rules didn't always apply. It made me think, especially after what Cut Glass said about Artistoneux and Pythagorus a few days ago.

I find all this fascinating. I suspect the point he was driving at was that truth is stranger than we might suppose.

He reckons three words should help us in making judgements about the world around us. He talked about the *'form'* society takes and how communities are organised to make a society. He talked about the *'orientation'* of society and how it is developing. Finally he talked about the *'forces'* within society, holding people together.

---

[20] E Abbott, Flatland, Seeley & Co (1880)

Form, orientation and force. I like that.

He described 'force' as being like gravitational waves and explained physics had only recently discovered them. The professor said these are like the energy connecting the universe. It's a powerful image. I can see it might be useful in thinking about the forces that connect people, the forces that connect me to Pearl.

Actually he made me think about some talks I went to a few years ago. Each was given by a leading politician from the Conservatives, from Labour and from the Liberals. They were all about about 'Good Society'

I took Jonathan from the London office to the third one.

We went for pizza on Mill Bank beforehand. I told him to listen out for the phrase 'little platoons' and how the speaker would refer to this quote, 'love the little platoons we belong to' and talk about the need for a 'a partnership not only between those who are living' but also with, 'those who are dead, and those who are to be born'[21] And they would say communities shouldn't be whipped into a frenzy by 'selfish and mischievous ambition'[22]

It's ironic, not long after I went to those talks, students smashed up the pizza restaurant in a riot because they felt politicians had betrayed them.

I am digressing. It's just that thoughts are colliding and spilling onto the page.

Tonight the professor introduced three speakers the Earl of Elstern who he described as an old friend, the Bishop of Saxby who he presented as something of a curiosity and the third speaker, presented as a lesser mortal on account of him being a medical scientist. This third speaker looked like the waiter in the cafe in Minister Square with his curly hair and Groucho Marx moustache.

I noticed that all the speakers talked around a common mantra that had this phrase at its heart: 'Respect the autonomous individual'. In their different ways, they each told us what 'well-being' and 'society' meant and gave us jelly-mould thoughts in varying colours.

'Respect the autonomous individual', felt an empty phrase.

Each speaker justified it saying, individuals should have the freedom to take responsibility for their lives and to make their own choices.

---

[21] Reflections on the French Revolution, Edmund Burke, J.M. Dent & Sons Ltd,1955, (Everyman edition),

[22] Reflections on the French Revolution, Edmund Burke, J.M. Dent & Sons Ltd,1955, (Everyman edition),

The thing is, I doubt I'm really free to make many choices on my own. I used to think I was. Now I'm really not so sure I've quite the freedom the speakers suggested.

I'm thinking about the black leather jacket I once bought. I thought a bit of a bobby-dazzler, but went to the Ring O' Bells and found every other man my age seemed to be wearing one. How much autonomy was there in my choice of jacket really?

So how much autonomy is involved in our choices, our freedom? Like Eli in the pub believing in vegan werwolves. Say it enough and you might come to believe they exist.

There's a dark side to all this. If we become used to thinking in certain ways, we call it 'common sense'. But it's not common sense. It's just the way everyone is thinking. It's two dimensional rules. I suppose this is where the professor's shift in perspective from the parallel lines to circles on a sphere fits in?

What people call common sense is just convention. What people are used to. Common sense can only be what's true all the time, everywhere and available to everyone. Buying the same black leather jacket is just adopting a convention. It's not common sense.

I'm imagining a hall of mirrors in a fairground. In one I look short and fat, in another I look tall and thin, in a third I look as I am. If all we have is a reflection, how do we know the truth, or is truth just what we see in a mirror at a particular time?

How do I know what's true?

There's something else I want to write down from tonight.

It occurred to me when my mind wandered, as I listened to the last speaker. My eyes wandered across the royal coat of arms hangs above the judge's seat in the Old Court House. It has a motto I've known all my life. - *Dieu et mon droit.* - 'God and My Right'. - People assume it's Latin. It's Norman French, the language of English kings after the Conquest. It's the king's battlecry that became a motto.

I suppose that motto is at the root of how things are. We've seen layers build up like layers of sand from the days of those Norman French kings. The first conquered. We think of William beating Harold and that was that, done and dusted. That's not how it was. People round here were smashed, starved, decimated in the Harrying of the North. Invaders came. They brought their own language. There's the evidence of it: a Norman French motto.

It took years to work through differences, to bury the injury. It's summed up in the ordering of things, in the battling out with the barons, in working out this idea of partnership in society, summing it up in Magna Carta.

Thinking about Magna Carta, I remember the business school dean I met. He was some kind of evangelical Christian who thought God wouldn't bless England if it forgot the principles of the Magna Carta. In fact, he confided he thought he'd get sacked if the university found he held these views. I thought him stupid and let him know! I asked him which magna carta he meant. He got in a tangle. He didn't know his history. He didn't know, there was a long, slow working through, layer on layer. I think the layers are still being laid down.

It's all too easy to see 'Respect the autonomous individual' as a battlecry. It seems to me, its a battlecry of the deluded. Self Law, autonomy doesn't exist. It can't. All it does is make someone alone.

I like that other sentence 'respect the connected individual'. That's a key to unlock what contributes to well-being in society. It takes time and working together.

That said it's ironic, I'm thinking and writing this alone in my Cupola room.

Day 29

That little mantra, 'respect the autonomous individual', has been on my mind.

I really like the idea of 'form', 'orientation' and 'force', holding society together.

If individuals go off to do as they please, what happens to the force that connects?

I read about Quantum Entanglement ages ago, how particles might be separated by unimaginable distances yet always spin in sync with one another. I'm no expert but it seems to me connecting forces can't be broken.

I went to the second-hand bookshop in Micklegate for a browse today. I bought a copy of The Prince. Someone had underlined this sentence:
> "Everyone sees what you appear to be, few experience what you really are"[23].

I last heard those words from the mouth of that retired admiral in his blazer and slacks at that development programme for 'senior leaders'. It's funny looking back, they were supposed to get people together from all walks of life to think about 'real world problems'. I think it was the establishment getting together for mutual back-slapping.

There was a colonel on the programme. I called him, Colonel Blimp. He stuck in my mind. I don't know why because I didn't like him. We barely exchanged a word. In fact, we circled like tomcats. I couldn't help turning the colonel into one of my cartoons, with his puffed out cheeks, a nose pointed upwards and a nipped in arse that made him swagger. We were in the same syndicate group with its facilitator called Jane.

Jane told us she was a Psychotherapist.

In the group, Jane kept referencing the empty chair to her right and told to imagine inviting our best selves to sit in the chair, so we could share our best qualities with the group.

Jane talked about FIRO Theory.[24] She didn't want me to talk about it. She kept stopping me. She talked about FIRO Theory as if it was FIRO Fact. She shut me up asking, 'Are you high functioning asperges?'. I wonder why she'd say such a thing?

---

[23] N. Machiavelli, The Prince, Penguin (2003)

[24] Schutz, W.C. (1958). FIRO: A Three Dimensional Theory of Interpersonal Behaviour. New York, NY: Holt, Rinehart, & Winston.

She wanted us to think about the importance of deliberate, reasoned choices. I've heard that so many times; too many times. I become less and less convinced each time I hear it.

Izzy at the office, constantly pumps out similar arguments he's read in some book.

The older I get, the more I think it's just bollocks.

I'm calling to mind the philosopher's question (I think they call it a syllogism), 'Are all ravens black?'. It's always made me smile. I know, the point of the question is that we can't know all ravens are black, we can only be likely to believe all ravens are black based all ravens we've ever come across being black.

I keep trying to tell Izzy he's wrong. So far, I don't think I've convinced him.

Maybe he just has to learn it.

There's a poem I always want to share with him, but I think it might go over his head. It has these words:
> *"It is unbecoming in a courteous man*
> *to try and to test but to trust no truth*
> *beyond those facts which flatter his judgement."* [25]

For me they're beyond, 'seeing is believing'.

It's ironic because I know that's the kind of saying that trips off the tongue. The thing is, it's only half the saying. The other half is always missed off:
> *'Seeing is believing, but feeling is the truth.'* [26]

I know the routine. I know the mantra about weighing evidence and all of that.

I suppose I'm just wondering how much of what I call truth is really just like an impression in wet sand, perhaps not even that. Maybe it's just my interpretation of that impression.
For example, why I didn't like Colonel Blimp? I can't think of any facts I can draw on to account for not liking him. There was just something about him I didn't like.

I contrast him with Hugh, Jane's marionette of the syndicate group. A clergyman, he was small with a sucked in bottom lip and nervous tick. He made fevered interjections into the group; more ejaculations than interjections.

---

[25] Armitage, S., Pearl, Faber & Faber (2017)

[26] Fuller T.,

Writing that made me laugh out loud. - I wonder if he might have suppressed Tourette's? - Jane, indulged Hugh. I suspect she flattered herself she could manipulate him or maybe simply perceived he would flatter her. Anyway, when Hugh wanted to speak, he'd clamber to the edge of his armchair and throw declarations into the group. I admit, I enjoyed listening to him.

By a strange coincidence, he talked about Jim the shagging minister from Patience St Congregational Street church. He referred to him as Jamie and told the group he was an advisor to the Archbishop of Canterbury.

When I knew Jim, he shagged Shagging Sheila the Sunday School Teacher and was defrocked. She carried on shagging. I really don't know which seduced the other, although I can guess.

I don't know if Sheila's husband knew anything. I think these days they'd call him a snowflake, wrapped up in himself. In the old days they'd call him a 'cuckold', with everyone knowing. They say he has a flat in Canary Wharf and who knows what goes on there. There are rumours.

Does it matter if Adulterous Jim became Virtuous Jamie?

Does it matter that Sheila's husband is cuckold or promiscuous, or that Sheila is a shagger?

Of course it matters!

I'm not sure what I think about Colonel Blimp. I sat across the room from him and felt uncomfortable about his beige chinos, oxford brogues and polo shirt with the collars standing up. I imagine he looked back at me thinking, 'middle-class, artsy, tree-hugger in cheesecloth and beige chinos'. I've not a single reason to suppose Blimp was any more or less trustworthy than Hugh. It's just how I felt at the time.

To get back to Machiavelli.

So how comes Pearl 'dresses like a hooker'? I can't fathom it, except I know her. I know who she is.

Day 30

An invitation to Kevin's funeral was on the doormat when I arrived home.

These words are printed on the front in gold type:
As needles point towards the pole,
When touched by the magnetic stone;
So faith in Jesus, gives the soul
A tendency before unknown.[27]

Mr Linn, Kevin's father has written a note across one corner in the shaky hand-writing of an old man. He says he'd love to see me after so many years.

I feel touched he should invite me, never mind write such a lovely note.

It is beyond question. I'll go. Tom will be there. It'll be strange meeting at the funeral

Important as the invitation is, I want to reflect on my journey home this evening. It's given me a lot to think about.

I caught the 18.33 from Kings Cross. The bishop was in the same carriage. That surprised me. Normally he's in First Class. Another bishop told me, it goes to their head when they take a seat in the Lords. He looked uncomfortable. That didn't surprise me. The woman in the next seat was chatting loudly. Chatting is an understatement! I couldn't help chuckling

He gripped his copy of the Telegraph like a shield.

Every now and then he'd lower his shield and sneak a look. His face flushed red and then turned pale. Oh the joy! Tides of intense emotions.

I had to get a closer look. I walked down the carriage. He looked up at me over half-moon spectacles. Pale blue eyes offered a plea-laden glimmer of acknowledgement.

I couldn't help myself 'good evening, bishop' and, 'How are you?' I gloated.

He winced. I enjoyed that.

In his thin and throaty voice he muttered a response I couldn't quite catch.

I said 'Pardon?', feigning warmth.

---

[27] J Newton, The Lodestone,

I felt none.

The women hemmed him in. Bosoms and folds of flesh spilled out of sequinned, stretched t-shirts. The one beside the bishop shovelled pasty into her mouth. She leapt from her seat as she saw me and lunged at me, pasty fell from full lips that attached limpet-like to mine.

It was Donna.

She was engineer of the bishop's dismay. What could I do but respond. From the corner of my eye, I saw his horror. I thought, 'just wait 'till she takes her teeth out'.

A couple squeezed by, dodging Donna's backside which acted as a counter-weight to the hugging end.

After escaping Donna's clutches, I found the couple had taken the seats opposite mine.

They were like characters from a 1940s costume drama but with hair dye.

He was whey-faced and spare with curling black hair that was relaxed more than unkempt. He wore black patent Dr Martin's with yellow laces, an over-sized, grey worsted suit and a burgundy cardigan. He settled to reading Keats. It suited him. He looked for all the world a delicate poet. I recognised him. I think he recognised me. He was the young man who was not the busker from the cafe in Minister Square.

She was dressed from neck to knee in floral print, a cashmere pashmina round her shoulders. She wore bright red Dr Martin's with yellow laces. Her hair was dyed purple. It tumbling round a fresh face, lit by a bright smile. She made notes from a book. Time and again she drew what remained of picked finger nails across bare forearms covered in red slashes. Some were raw.

She glanced from her book to me and back to her book. He read Keats and paid me no regard.

Donna and her friends were opening cans of lager.

The bishop cast me a desperate glance.

I wonder if the bishop would write about his train journey in his weekly blog or refer to it in Thought for the Day on Radio Four. I wonder what he'd say? I'm with the professor the other night. This particular bishop is a grand-standing curiosity.

It sounds a small thing, but I heard someone say a new bishop 'should buy his own sausages'.[28] I'm with them.

I like that charge to a new bishop, 'They should buy their own sausages'. It feels a bit like 'Let them eat cake' as a declaration about starting people, but opposite.

I suppose in a way it was sad watching this one hiding behind his paper.

I guess it's easier to be with pretty people reading poetry.

Mind you, even if we'd swapped places and talked about Keats but I doubt he'd have understood. He'd discuss the poetry and miss the tragedy. That's the irony of the Romantics; scrubbed-clean isn't Keats.

.

---

[28] Church Times, June 21st 2019, Wilkinson, P.

Day 31

I bumped into Sean today.

Being Tuesday and market day, I wandered through the stalls to the Buttercross on my way to the cafe.

I wouldn't have noticed him in his priest's get up. When I see him in the Ring O' Bells he's always in a baggy jumper and jeans. We sat together on a bench under the Buttercross.

The busker was in his usual place under the corner arch. He's really good. I'd not noticed before but his guitar is very small. I don't know why, I never expected such a small guitar.

I told Sean about Nathaniel Ayton and Daniel Defoe meeting under the Buttercross. He seemed interested. Thinking about it now, I feel a bit of an insensitive idiot. I should've remembered Nathaniel and Daniel were protestants wanting to fight catholics.

There's always been something undisclosed about Sean. He told me a bit of his story so I feel I've gotten to know Sean better.

I hate that word 'gotten' being treated as an americanism. We've given it to the Americans. We should claim it back.

It seems Sean's dad was a drinker who beat his mum. She escaped to a refuge in Sheffield.

Apparently it was the Mother's Union, the Church of England's paramilitary who spirited this poor woman and her boy away.

I wouldn't have thought they'd get involved. I've been allergic to them since they came to see mum that time. All I saw was what grandma called 'stiff women', sitting in the drawing room drinking tea, eating cake and leaving Sombre Sympathy. It just shows how you can get the wrong impression.

It turns out she moved from the refuge to a bedsit in the top of someone's house on Victoria Road. Then out of desperation she went on the game in Broomhall.

It's easy to make judgements. Who'd want to be a hooker on the streets?

I walked through Broomhall once. I was heckled by hookers.

I always imagined catholic priests went in as boys from well-scrubbed homes and carried on until they croaked.

Sean ran away to be a boy soldier and was nearly blown up on County Antrim during the Troubles in Northern Ireland.

I knew lads from school who joined up and were sent to Northern Ireland. I can't begin to imagine what they went through.

I remember meeting that Irish catholic bus driver in Manchester who told me the first thing he saw when he arrived from Ireland was a statue of Oliver Cromwell. He knew he was in a hostile place.

We think sectarianism is dead.

I remember divides when I was young; whispered references of 'they're catholics you know'.

I've been to St George's Market in Belfast. They have street food and live music now.

Thinking about Sean and me, looking over the market in Saxby and hearing the busker, I couldn't help thinking, we've had our share of fanatics under the Buttercross.

From our bench under the Buttercross, we saw someone we supposed was a beggar not far from the busker. Almost idly Sean said, 'With my dog collar, I can speak to more of less anyone. It doesn't mean I'm accepted any more than that beggar.'

I gave to a beggar outside Liverpool Street station. I felt sorry for him. He was well spoken and had been a soldier in Afghanistan.

Oh and I chatted to one outside the supermarket in St Paul's Street in Leeds. I don't know why I spoke to him. We chatted quite nicely really. It surprised me. He said he was from Wales and liked being on the street. He said he had a tent somewhere in Headingley. I couldn't get my head around it.

Sean and I parted under the Buttercross. He walked off in the direction of the Minster. I walked to the cafe for my coffee and almond croissant.

I sat at my table in the window watching the stout woman selling her cheese. No more than five feet tall and as wide as she is tall, I there's something about her.

I bought plums from the fruit stall.

I laugh at myself when I eat plums. I arrange the stones in a line on my plate, each touching its neighbour. I count them with that rhyme, 'Tinker, tailor, solider, sailer, rich man, poor man, beggar-man, thief.' We did that at home. We'd put the stones from plum crumble round our plates and count them off. It's the '*beggar-man, thief*' part that strikes home.

In the old days, if you were a neighbour you were known and bound to those around you. If you weren't a neighbour you were a stranger, no better than a beggar-man or a thief. It's funny that, Sean thinks a priest is little different to a beggar-man or a thief.

I don't know my neighbours, still less feel bound to them.

Be that as it may, before I go to bed I want to write about the dream I had last night. It's been at the back of my mind all day.

There were three foul ogres pressing against me with slimy, sweating bodies dribbling spittle. Worse, there was a bishop who looked like death. He prowled and snarled through grinning slavering smiles. He'd disappear, leaving just a disembodied mouth with its cynical smile.

The mouth kept forming the word 'marvellous' with menacing repetition through red, quivering lips from behind the ogres. I couldn't hear him say it but somehow I knew that's what he was saying.

I wonder what Sean would make of that!

The dream had me tossing and turning. I wanted to get some air, so I went outside to to sit where I am now, here on the terrace.

There was a treat in the early hours. He comes about this time every year, to sing for his lover. In the quiet, I could just hear him.

Now as I write, these words spring to mind, crystallising a thought:
> *Darkling I listen; and, for many a time*
> *I have been half in love with easeful Death,*

I can't help thinking I feel caught in an in-between place, not so much between stranger and neighbour as between alone and abandoned. It's a bit depressing really after all the work I've put into life, but I suppose I feel more and more a stranger in my own world.

No-one out there would think my life would feel like this: abandoned!

That thought has more or less bounced me to the church in Adder's Wynd. It's boarded up and sprayed with graffiti. It's not a place to be after dark. I passed it on my way to Scarab today. I suppose it's on my mind.

131

I know two stories of how Adder's Wynd got its name. I'm not sure which is true. (I know a third but doubt that's true.)

One says, 'adder' comes from 'alder' meaning, 'eagle', the symbol for St John the Evangelist. The other says 'alder' is a shortened form of 'St Aethelbert', the Anglo-Saxon king who the Normans tried to scrub out after the Conquest.

I like the story about St Aethelbert best. Whichever, 'Adder' is engraved like graffiti in the memory of the wynd.

Actually 'wynd' is a strange relic word of this place. It's a winding back street or a little lane.

I love Scarab's design. It's simple, powerful and almost primal; an echo of something.

I'm going to take a couple of days to be sure I want to go through with it. I'm fairly certain I will.

Day 32

I went to Cavendish's in Stonegate when I was in York today. I wanted to buy something to mark my, whatever it is with Pearl. I bought a ring. It's silver with a red quartz stone surrounded by marquisette. It's only costume jewellery. It's a gesture. I hope she'll like it. The lady who served me put it in a green box.

On the train home, I wrote a note and hid it in the box lid. As I wrote, I heard a little voice whispering, 'words are for those with promises to keep'[29]. I intend to keep them. I know words can be fickle. I don't intend to be fickle.

Steve and Chris and probably everyone else would think my commitment signals 'frisson', tryst', 'infatuation'. I don't care.

I called in at the Ring O' Bells before I went home. I thought Steve and Chris might've been in. They weren't but I bumped into Dominic. He hasn't changed since he worked for me. He looked like a weasel back then. He looks like a weasel now, all spindly and jaundice looking with his wispy, straggly brown hair, goaty and narrow, over-wide eyes that seem to be constantly sliding from side to side.

I haven't seen him in years. I tried to be civil. That said I was aware my handshake gripped that little bit too firmly and for too long. I don't deny I enjoyed the feeling that came with my grip. I didn't enjoy the feel of his over-long, cold, boney, jaundiced grip against mine.

I went to the bar and chatted to Eli. Evidently she'd noticed my encounter with Dominic. 'What's with you and Dominic?', she asked.

I said, 'It was nothing'. I'm not sure she believed me.

Eli told me Dominic had been with The Derricks at the other end of the bar. I nodded to them. They nodded back.

I watched them.

Eli danced and sang to herself.

I entertained myself with images of dive bars and confrontations. I like the idea of a rough pub with real people. The Ring O' Bells is as close as you get to that in Saxby.

I still want to spell Eli's name E-L-L-I-E.

---

[29] Their Lonely Betters, W H Auden, Poems Selected by John Fuller, Faber & Faber (2000)

She intrigues me.

She appears open, fresh and innocent. She's very small and has to stand on her toes to pull my pint.

I hadn't noticed before. She's a beautiful tattoo on her left arm. - I wouldn't have noticed something like that a few weeks ago. - It's a bunch of forget-me-nots and butterflies.

I have learned tattoos can be very personal. I asked about it.

She told me she often goes for walks in Hobbe Wood and sees swathes of forget-me-nots amongst the hazel and the alder. Apparently she watches butterflies on the flowers as spring turns to summer. She called them 'pretty things in dark places.'

With that she was off to serve The Derricks.

I watched them letch at her, eyes reaching over the bar to touch her.

Humpty-back Derrick pretended not to look.

Sanctimonious Derrick pressed himself closer to the bar.

I admit, she has a lovely arse. What they were doing was a bit shabby.

Humpty-Back is a magistrate and twisted personally and physically He's an elder at Patience Street Congregational church. I know he tried to cover up for Jim, the shagging minister blaming it all on Shagging Sheila the Sunday School teacher.

Sanctimonious was bankrupt for fiddling his taxes. I remember being unsure about him but tried to do a good turn by giving him some work. He insisted on being paid in cash and refused to give a receipt.

I can't think what they'd have to do with Dominic.

I can't think why we call them the Derricks. I think it's got something to do with them being miserable bastards, ripping people up and hanging them out to dry if they don't agree with them.

Anyway, why do the Derricks suppose they have the right to take from Eli with their look. What she has isn't theirs to take.

Eli came back to me and said she thinks The Derricks are a pair of 'raincoat wankers'.

I spluttered beer trying to stop myself laughing,

134

Her eyes blinked and me.

I could've sworn her tits swelled across the bar and her jeans grew that bit tighter along with her pert red lips becoming that bit more full.

I wonder if the Derricks watched me and thought I was letching.

I don't think I was.

I didn't mean to.

She held me, not the other way round.

She plunged me into empty silence. She broke it, grabbing my satchel and pulling the scarf out. Draping it round her neck, she danced along the bar.

She teased me, 'Tell me who she really is, Mr Zombie from the house in Hobbe Wood. Is she the Object of your Desire?'.

She turned 'Object of Desire', into a noun and an accusation.

I was aware The Derricks were looking from Eli to me and back again.

I couldn't stop her dancing and waving the scarf around.

The Derricks focus stayed with me.

She handed the scarf back with two hands, almost reverentially.

Out of the blue Eli told me a story I hadn't expected. It was this:
> An atheist met the Pope and said, 'Searching for God is like looking for a
> non-existent black cat in a room with no light while blindfold.'. The Pope
> responded saying, 'The cat found me'.[30]

She explained how she'd been feeling for truth in the darkness but the truth found her when she wasn't looking.

I confess I wasn't sure where this would go, given our previous conversation about vegan werwolves in the woods.

---

[30] https://www.youtube.com/watch?v=GS3BZs5fx3Q

Pointing to a butterfly in her tattoo, she told me the truth came to her watching a butterfly on forget-me-nots.

I confess, I thought, 'Here we go. We're in werewolf territory'.

She'd heard how a butterfly beating its wings can change the course of a tornado. For her the thought a fragile, beautiful butterfly changing something epic struck home.

She blinked at me across the bar and handed the scarf back saying, 'It's obvious she's not an object of desire'.

I hope Eli is right. I don't want Pearl to be an object of desire in any sense I can recognise. There's just that something we have.

I've been taking a moment to look at the ring I bought in Cavendish's. No, that's not quite right. The truth is, I took a moment to dally with the green box, rolling it round with my finger tips and just wondering. At the most basic level, its just a bit of pretty costume jewellery that cost very little but I hope she'll like. Yet, I'm also happy for it to cost me all I have.[31]

It's funny, a sentence has floated from the back of my mind that I need to write down. 'I am no better than my fathers'.[32] It feels a digression, to be off the point but I'm not sure that's so. It's one of those little sayings that surfaces for me every now and then. I know it's words from the mouth of someone who'd run away and had to face up to himself, to what he must do.

I think I am coming to understand.

---

[31] Matthew 13:45-46

[32] 1Kings 19:4

Day 33

Thinking about my conversation in the pub with Eli last night has led to an epiphany.

I wonder, am I so different to The Derricks?

I want to be.

There's so much I want to be.

In fact, in my heart I sense a new adventure, that will have me leave this Cupola room.

The thing is, I love this house. I've loved it from the moment I walked through the door on my first viewing. I'm at peace here. It's my safe haven. It always will be. So why would I want to be anywhere else?

There were all kinds of stories about the house having been a haunt for highwaymen when it was a coaching inn, about it being a watchtower for Saxby centuries ago and about Lilburne billeting his vanguard here before their march to Elsternwick.

I couldn't give it up.

Views from the gardens are incredible, overlooking Hobbe Wood and the gorge and then away over the estuary. It's always struck me how the woods must have been an impenetrable tangle of hazel and alder for any enemy. Doubtless the stories of them being haunted by hobgoblins would've been one more defence, never mind Eli's zombie's and vegan werewolves.

Enough of that. I want to think about my day.

I walked home along Long Wall and sat on a bench for a few minutes to enjoy the view of the marina. The bench had one of those a little memorial plaques. It read, '*To Claude and Madge. They enjoyed this place'.* I can just imagine an old couple holding hands through the decades and taking their evening walk to that spot. It's a nice thought.

The word 'enjoyed' shouted at me.

I'm going to get a bit anal for a moment. EN-JOY-ED. ED puts enjoy in the past. It's what Claude and Madge did on the bench. EN has them making their joy there. But just what is this thing called JOY?

It's more than happy.

It's more than pleasure.

I guess you know it when you know it.

How would it be if joy was the flip side of sorrow, just as fear is the flip side of hope?

Jonathon Ayton said life is a Labyrinth of Sorrows. How would it be if life was a Labyrinth of Joy instead? How would that work?

I like the idea.

Anyway, I'm just thinking about the marina Claude and Madge looked over from their Bench of Joy. It's a pretty view now. It wasn't always so.

I don't suppose there was much joy when the saxons came and after them the vikings with all their raping and pillaging. Then there was William the Conquerer paying the off Danes in his Harrying of the North. I remember reading how William committed genocide. They say a hundred thousand died in Yorkshire on account of his cruelty. Bloody Normans!

The marina looks idyllic now. I guess we decorate over history.

I'm not sure why but I felt the need to hold onto the little lodestone on my keyring as I walked home from Claude and Madge's Bench of Joy. I notice, I've given it that title and not just described the bench as having that effect.

Mr Linn was right when he gave us each a lodestone. Holding it helps me find direction. I know it's nothing really. I find it helpful. So why not? Why not hold fast to beliefs that are helpful.

My keys are downstairs by the door. I could do with going down to grab hold of them right now, so I can hold onto my lodestone and think about my new adventure.

Day 34

I've put the CD on again. I play it when I can. I love to think the songs have been so carefully chosen for me. Anyway, there we are.

Let me begin by writing about my walk home tonight.

Hobbe Syke felt eerily silent on my walk home. In amongst the shady gloom, I couldn't help noticing the tumbling swathes of blue around the trees and the railings. Forget-me-not. They made me think of Eli. They were happy thoughts urging me to put on my boyish self and run along the railings doing my stick thing, making that clattering sound. No-one could see and I doubt anyone listened.

I've learned, I need to find a place to let rip every now and then. There's no harm. It reminds me I'm just a boy.

Right up until Alzheimer's took hold, mum would look at me with a twinkle in her bright blue eyes and say, '*To you I might be an old woman, but inside I'm just a girl*'. She became that girl more and more on the outside. I won't forget being with her in that..........I wanted to write, 'that decline'.........but I am not sure it was 'decline'. She sheds the old woman and lives a girl again.

My stick clattering along the railings is about me, a boy again, with mischievous joy. I love it.

Mum is locked in the girl she was, I'm still a man, reaching for that moment of joy.

The clatter of the stick a noisy, grown up *'fuck off, fuck off, fuck off'*, chasing fear away, along the shadowy syke in the woods.

I guess that's what mum's girl did, she chased the terror of Alzheimers away, as a rich life collapsed into numb confusion.

I passed the Bench of Joy on my way home. It made me think about another Claude. Claude Shotton. He was the Sunday School Superintendent when I was a boy.

I remember him being older than dad. He lived in a cottage down Pinfold Lane, just along from Pearl's house. I an almost hear his strange, high-pitched voice. I remember hi as an odd little man who lived with his brother.

He was odd with Pearl. I remember he always wanted her 'where he could see her' and had her sit close to him on the front row in Sunday School. I've no idea why.

He didn't seem to like Pearl being close to anyone else, at least no other adult. I've no idea why at the time.

Doris played the piano in Sunday school. We didn't have hymn books. All the words were on a flip chart.

Mr Shotton seemed to live for being Sunday School Superintendent.

I don't think I was a good lad, always far more concerned with what was in the store cupboard and with Janet Field's budding tits.

I've not thought about Janet for years. She was tiny, with wild ginger hair and a reputation to go with it. God, I remember when the two of us went up to the Pinfold. How old would I have been, maybe sixteen?

The song playing on the CD is an odd one. It's unlike the others; an unlikely choice really. I don't know why but this line has caught my attention:
"With the holy water in her hand, she cast the compass round"[33]
It's reminded me of the story of the wronged, innocent girl who had the courage to reach out and save her bewitched lover. I can just about remember it, but the thought is forcing me to make bizarre connections I want to push away.

I remember the girl in the story, the girl in the song I suppose was called Janet.

It's making me think of Janet.

She was certainly very willing. She was known for being willing.

That Sunday school storage cupboard fascinated me. There was all sorts in there: stirrup pumps, rolled up rope ladders, old blackout curtains and folded tarpaulins. There was that smell that was just old.

I wonder if Janet was generous and giving, or whether we took from her?

I digress.

Anyway, back to Claude Shotton. He always seemed so frustrated with us lads. We made fun of him behind his back, trying to mimic his half-broken voice when ours hadn't broken.

He'd get cross with us and his voice would go beyond falsetto. We'd laugh the way lads do. Frustrated he'd say, 'Will I ever get through to ya'. Mind all o'wert shop.'

---

[33] Steeleye Span,- Tam Lin - Label Shanachie (1991)

We'd sit in one of those little alcoves to one side of the bottom Sunday School room. Mr Shotton, would talk about life. I can remember him getting us all to think about life and what we'd like to become. We'd only be ten or eleven, but I can remember the conversation so clear.

Mr Shotton told us about the way we might find direction in our lives. The word he used as come back to me, 'god-ness'. He talked about the little bit of 'god-ness' inside us that should always tell us the difference between doing a good thing or a bad thing and that the test was whether what we did built someone else up or tore them down.

I suppose his lesson stuck. I remembered it, even though it was at the back of my mind. I'm challenged to think about the way I direct, the way I orientate my life. I'm not sure I've always been that good.

I don't think they teach such things these days.

Actually I wonder if life sometimes sees us snuff out that little bit of god-ness, so we end up focusing just on what we want. No. So I've focused on what I've wanted.

It's may be a bit extreme, but I'm back with Janet Field at the Pinfold where all we wanted was what felt good.

My mind has jumped to that time I stood on the threshold of Pearl's bedroom. It wouldn't have been that long after Janet at the Pinfold. I knew not to go in.

I wonder why I only did what was right with just one of them?

I'm forced to look back and join the dots of my life, I wonder what's been grace and what's been virtue?

It's not to do with my journal really but I saw something today that really struck a chord. I passed a young mum with her little child crossing Minster Square. I heard the child say, 'I have got a skip inside me' as she skipped along. I watched her mum join in with the skipping. They skipped in and out of the Buttercross, between the arches. They seemed oblivious to the world around them. Isn't that just the point: to live like that child, to be innocent and oblivious. Isn't that when grace and joy come out to play? It certainly has it's appeal.

141

Day 35

I've learned the names of the people at the café in Minister Square, Aperitivo! They are Frankie and Maria. I know this because Carolyn joined me for coffee. It was a complete surprise to see her. She phoned me at work. I've no idea how she knew where I worked.

I only learned the name of the cafe a few days ago, never mind the names of the people who own it. How is it Carolyn got to know such detail so easily?

The waiter is known to everyone in Saxby as the 'Singing Waiter'. It seems his real name is Frankie. He's small with wiry, grey hair and that thick, thick moustache. I thought I'd better put the second 'thick' for emphasis. It's his dominant feature and has a life of its own. Apparently, he's from Milan. I wish I'd known that before. I love Milan.

The waitress is Maria. She's American. I knew that. She's very direct and brusque. I knew that too. I'd already guessed New York. Carolyn confirms she's from the Bronx and is Frankie's wife. Evidently, Frankie collected her in transit from Milan; although personally I can't imagine this Maria being 'collected' by anyone. She seems her own person to me. Anyway, I'm sure Carolyn is better at knowing these things than me.

When Carolyn was chatting to Maria, I tried and join in, but I can be clumsy when I don't know the protocol. I was quite excited to hear Marie talk with passion about New York. Because I've been, I blurted out a question and then felt awkward. I asked if she knew Caffe Falai in Lafayette Street. She does! I'll never forget going there. David Bowie was at the next table.

I noticed when Carolyn spoke with both Frankie and Maria: she focused on the person speaking more than what was said. I always focus on what's said. I think I miss out.

Carolyn still has an ocean of blond hair, which she flicks as a reflex when she laughs. She laughs often and her eyes shimmer mesmerising green.

When we were young I looked up to Carolyn. She was 'above my pay grade', with no pretence, no affectation. Yet, if I'm honest with myself she was always a little bit, over there in the corner watching. She was confident, for sure. I'm not sure what it was. It may not have been anything really. There was just something about her way; just a little bit distant I suppose. She was gracious and lovely though.

When we were young, she'd to refer to Pearl as 'Little Miss Margaret'. I remember her coming to see me, after I walked away that night. I've never forgotten. Apparently, she'd seen it all and watched me storm off after Tom had tried to argue with me. I remember standing in the kitchen the next morning, feeling cut up about

143

what had happened. I looked out of the window and Carolyn was walking down the drive. She'd come to see me to tell me I'd been cruel. I think I knew that really, but I was so full of myself back then, I couldn't go back. I remember her saying, 'That wasn't very chivalrous Sir Gawain'.

She used to call me Sir Gawain. She called me by that today. I've no idea why. It feels a bit random.

It was lovely to see her. She hasn't changed. She's beautiful: gentle, warm and insightful.

Over coffee, I told her about my Cupola room and this journal.

She listened intently, eye's sparkling, holding me.

I babbled.

I don't think anyone would think me a babbler.

How is it she has that effect on me?

She's always been able to see right through me.

She's always known when I'm talking rubbish and has that certain gesture. She holds her hands in front of her, wrings them for a moment and gently puts them, one on top of the other on the table, or on my knee or wherever. Then she simply says, 'Well anyway Mr Bran', or 'Well anyway, Sir Gawain'. That shuts me up. She did that in the kitchen after I'd I walked away from Pearl.

She did it to abate my babbling this afternoon, stopping me in full flow.

It was just the same when she took me for that drink in her Ford Mustang; when she told me 'Miss Debs' wasn't the right one.

A bit of me thinks she's just nosey, interfering in my relationships and that she ought to sort her own life out. I get the impression she always goes for the 'damaged goods' and never really commits. The truth is, I know she has my best interests at heart.

What is it they say of people like Carolyn.......High emotional intelligence, or something like that.

I really am a bit rubbish at all that touchy feely stuff.

I suppose she's a bit of a barometer; a good indicator of whether things are set fair or heading for stormy waters.

What's odd is that she's so protective, I've no idea why.

I know I babbled to Carolyn trying to confide that I don't really have a clue about my 'connection' with Pearl.

All she said in response was, 'Real relationships don't follow rules. Rules follow relationships'.

I'm not entirely sure what she meant. It felt like a kick in the balls.

It turned out Carolyn had arranged to meet just to make sure I was going to Kevin's funeral. How could I not! I told her that. When I said I was going, she did that other intense gesture of hers, narrowing her eyes and concentrating on me for what felt like too long and then simply saying 'I'm glad'.

I'm having another go at making sense of my world and what's going on. I'm looking up at the stars projected on my Cupola ceiling.

My thoughts are a bit muddled after my lovely time with Carolyn.

I'm taking a moment to take in the constellations projected on the cupola. I've always loved being up here, at the centre of my cosmos, spinning around my very own pole star.

Tonight I'm finding myself concentrating on the hunter, Orion.

I'm thinking about his story: his adventures; his loves and his lost loves and how he's trapped up there.

Orion's boast was to rid the earth of wild animals but his ambition was far beyond his capacity. The earth goddess, Gaia was angry and sent a scorpion to finish him off. So the story goes, Orion couldn't kill the scorpion, ran away and was accidentally killed by Artemis, the goddess of the hunt. The gods put his image in the sky to remind her of him.

Perhaps Orion also reminds us - reminds me - there's more than my own spinning cosmos, the limitation of my own rule, my own ways of seeing.[34]

Anyway I am going to get myself off to bed. I need to be up in good time to get ready for the funeral.

---

[34] Job 9:9, Job 38:31

Day 36

Today was brilliant. It's an odd word to describe a day dominated by a friend's funeral. It's the best word I can find.

Of course there was sadness. It just wasn't maudlin, except for that Father Michael and his banal sentimentality.

Sentimentality's not a bad thing in itself. We need some every now and then. I suppose it's just not me; not where I am.

We had these words:
> "Media vita in morte sumus", "in the midst of life we are in death".

A bit of me can see death is the last great adventure.

Who knows with certainty what's beyond that dark gateway from this life?

Anyway, Pearl and I went to wave Kevin off today. We met at Pullen Bridge and drove to the crematorium. We stood at the door with the others. Our whole life was there: waiting.

There was just one spray of flowers on the coffin. Lilacs. The funeral director opened the car door for Tom and Mr Linn and a woman I didn't know. She was ashen and faded, with the saddest eyes as I've ever seen.

Tom always had such a spare frame. He looked forlorn. Lost. I wonder if he's let go of his lodestone?

Tom, his father and the faded woman led us into the chapel.

Mr Linn smiled as he passed, reaching out his hand to touch mine. It was the slightest touch.

Two clergymen walked in front of Kevin's coffin, Father Francis and this Father Michael character. They swapped about at the front during the service. First it was one was, then the other, like characters in a Swiss clock. Evidently, this Father Michael is chaplain at the hospice where Kevin died. He gave a talk, explaining how he and Kevin had become friends. I wasn't convinced.

He began with a bit of Eliot:
> *April is the cruellest month, breeding*
> *Lilacs out of the dead land, mixing*

Memory and desire,[35]

He read as if they were his own words.

I think funeral eulogies need to be your own words.

Father Michael expanded on the theme of lilacs, telling us how he and Kevin looked out on the hospice garden and its Lilac tree. Evidently it reminded him of a similar tree in the garden of the house where he grew up. He told us how great wands of purple flowers grew and then faded but would come again each year. We knew this. He connected the flowers to our memories of Kevin. It was a nice image, if sentimental. I did wonder how often he'd trotted out the same banalities, tugging on the heart-strings of the grieving families to jerk a few tears.

I didn't want to hear about where the Father Michael grew up, or what he saw, or his feelings. I certainly didn't want sentimentality wrung from a poem that's not sentimental

I was cross with him. His talk was contrived. I judged his friendship feigned.

Father Francis spoke about how he and Mr Linn drank whiskey and cried together, knowing what it was to lose a son.

I smiled when Father Francis spoke of Kevin's 'roguish ways' and yet his 'serious care and chivalry'.

I brought the Order of Service home.

I read these words:
> *He is gracious and full of mercy.*
> *He is slow to anger and quick to show kindness.*
> *He does not deal with us according to our failings.*
> *He does not judge us as we deserve.*[36]

I can't help thinking Kevin was a better man than me.

Pearl and I walked out of the crematorium chapel just behind Tom, his Father and the faded lady. Our hands curled together. I can't remember doing that before. Her hand is soft and small; the hand of a child.

---

[35] Eliot T S, The Wasteland, The Burial of the Dead, The Selected Poems of T S Eliot, Faber & Faber, (1954)

[36] Psalm 103

148

Father Francis saw. He held his hand towards us. We loosed and I shook his. He and Pearl hugged as a father hugs a daughter.

Beyond him was Father Michael who held out a hand to shake. We shared a polite condolence.

I saw the faded lady, so evidently alone. People were all round her. None were with her. I watched, imagining who she was.

I think she must have been Jan. Kevin's 'Soulmate', 'the Love of His Life'. I remember him using those phrases as titles more than descriptions.

How sad.

Actually, when I think about the grievers, I was struck by something I've not noticed before. There seems a convention amongst men. They hug in a way they wouldn't at other times. They give generous, manly hugs that without exception end in three firm taps by the left hand of the hugger on the back of the right shoulder of the hugged. The last tap is immediately followed by a speedy release and a rapid push away. It's more a dance than a hug.

Tom and me; we hugged. It wasn't that man-hug of grief-sharing. We gripped each other and wept. I pulled his head into my neck. He pulled mine into his. This was an embrace not a hug. I felt his tears, moist and warm. We clung to each other, just for a moment.

These words are rolling round the back of my mind:
'Whatever we were to each other, that we still are.'[37]

They're not about Kevin. Not now. They're about Tom and me.

I'm thinking about the words Father Michael used.

I read them first years ago. They meant nothing then. They were just words to read.

I've found some more words from that poem. Father Michael didn't use these in the funeral:
"Shall I at least set my lands in order?"[38]

I like their challenge.

---

[37] H Scott Holland, All is Well, (1896)

[38] Eliot T S, The Wasteland, The Burial of the Dead, The Selected Poems of T S Eliot, Faber & Faber, (1954)

Day 37

I've had quite a day of it.

I'd like to be able to say I woke early and chose to go for a brisk walk, but I've no idea how I got myself to Finkle St. That's where Maria found me around four this morning.

I must've gone via my French windows, because they were wide open when Maria brought me home, but the front and back doors were locked. It's so out of character. I must have let myself out and walked down the garden and through the little wicket gate onto Hobbe syke. I've no memory of it.

What was I thinking of!

I vaguely recall something inside shouting, "STOP!", but I couldn't.

Things had been going round and round in my head all night.

It was just like this last year, when I was so stressed.

I'm so grateful to Maria. She saw me and brought me home, walking me all the way.

She made me coffee and sat with me.

We didn't talk.

I just sat.

Silent.

Nothing made sense.

I sat around more or less the whole day.

In fact I sat here in my chair by the French windows, barely moving a muscle.

It was as if I'd been tied down.

Before she left, Maria went the extra mile inviting me to what she called an *'Aperitivo'*, if I felt up to it. I promised to try and make myself go.

I'm writing this having just arrived back.

I'm so glad I kept my promise.

I set off, the same way I'd wandered out in the night. At more or less the point Maria found me on Finkle St, I came across a group of people. They looked lost. The old lady in the group was clearly tired. She reminded me of mum. I stopped to ask if they needed directions. I didn't like to think of her struggling. The man was about my age. He was assertive, but not in charge. The younger woman was in charge, but didn't know which direction to take. I suppose that sounds a bit of an oxymoron: in charge but not knowing which direction to take. Maybe she was just bossy and gave the impression of being in charge.

When I asked, it turned out they were heading for Minister Square. I offered to walk with them and took them down little St Saviour Gate, by the Minister.

I imagined him an accountant. I've no idea why I came to that conclusion. He wore a grey suit, Balliol college cuff-links and had a matching college tie. The younger woman, was precise and well turned out. She wore what grandma would've called a 'two piece' and had an array of jangly bangles and over-sized beads. I think the elderly lady was mother to one of the other two. She looked like she lived somewhere like the Burgages in Elsternwick and had a coat on that had seen better days. I assume her off-spring have done well for themselves! They should've bought her a new coat. It turned out they were going to the Aperitivo too. I explained we needed to walk across Minster Square and under the Buttercross.

Frankie saw us and opened his arms in welcome. We walked that little bit faster in response. He kept repeating in Italian and then English, '*Vieni, vieni, sei il benvenuto'* ("Come, come, you are very welcome"). At the door he ushered us inside. Forgetting himself, he spoke excitedly in Italian, '*Per favore unisciti a noi. Avere qualcosa da mangiare'* but forgot to translate - His warmth was infectious, the lack of translation, disconcerting.

The three of them hesitated for that millisecond of awkward.

I'd never been in the upstairs part of the café before today. Evidently it's a function room. This function - this Aperitivo - was to celebrate Frankie and Maria's son's engagement who turned out to be the whey-faced Keats reader from the train. His fiancée is the pretty girl with the cuts on her arms. She's Rachel.

The three of them - the people I came in with - went to sit at a table on the far side of the room. They looked uncomfortable.

I watched Frankie take an ancient woman across to them. Dressed in black and with iron-grey hair, she shuffled. Frankie spoke to her very loudly, '*Questo è il padre, la madre e la nonna di Rachel'* ('This is Rachel's father, mother and grandmother'). They stood to greet her. The old lady reached out her hands to Rachel's grandmother saying, 'Rachel è una bella ragazza, così delicata. *Devi* essere molto orgoglioso di tua nipote'.[39] She couldn't translate. She didn't need to. Rachel's grandmother recoiled slightly not understanding a word. Then she took her hands. No words were needed.

Frankie took me to meet those gathering round the long table overflowing with food down the middle of the room. I didn't know if I was in Saxby, New York or Milan. Most spoke very loudly and very quickly in Italian, or in that slightly nasally Brooklyn accent, or in what I call the 'posh Yorkshire'.

Actually they're a funny bred, the posh Yorkshire ones. I know even now nothing much happens without their say-so. It's not that they're the Saxby mafia or anything, but they are into everything; mostly old money or families who've been here for generations. They care about the place.

As the afternoon went on, Rachel's father had rather more Prosecco than is good for an accountant with college cufflinks and Rachel's grandma was exalted as 'nonna'. Only Rachel's mother held onto her lifeline of misplaced English propriety.

I felt for her.

She stood to one side of the room, resisting inducements to join in. I felt for her.

I'm glad I didn't resist today. I'm glad I accepted Maria's invitation.

Back in my armchair by the French windows in the quietness of my evening, I'm reflecting on what's been a rollercoaster of a day!

Last night I woke without the capacity to process my thoughts, a fog enveloping my chaos.

This afternoon I was caught up in kindness and struck by the two grandmothers, the two nonnas who understood without words.

It makes me think about yesterday at the funeral.

I'm thinking about when Tom and I hugged. I felt his tears. I think that's what got to me most. It felt right, as did that moment Pearl and I held hands leaving the crematorium chapel. There was an innocence. Isn't it strange how tiny gestures say so much.

I think what I'm taking from this difficult of rollercoaster day is about the innocence of touch and embrace.

---

[39] 'Rachel is a beautiful girl, so delicate. You must be very proud of your granddaughter'

153

I know there's so much talk today of inappropriate touching and the theft and abuse of something so important. It's just that right now at the end of my own day, I'm treasuring being touched and embraced by those beyond comfortable.

Day 38

I'm back in my armchair beside the French windows.

I still call them french windows.

When I had them fitted, the brochure described them as 'bi-fold doors'.

I thought they'd bring more light into the sitting room.

I prefer the old french windows, if I'm honest.

They reminded me of the ones we had at home.

I'm still feeling fragile.

I'm going to be really self-indulgent and write about simple things of no obvious consequence today, like the French windows and this armchair.

It doesn't fit in.

I almost didn't bring it from mum and dad's when I broke up their home.

I love this room's clean lines, with its cream sofas and terracotta tiled floor. It's beautiful in its simplicity.

This armchair isn't beautiful. It's a lumpy, squashy and the faded jacquard fabric has worn thin. It's just that it's stuffed with memories.

I love it. As I sat down tonight I noticed a corner of a piece of paper sticking out of the join between the back and the seat. I don't know why I haven't noticed it before. I managed to pull it out and discovered it was a guide to the chapel at Windsor. It's the kind of thing dad would've liked. He'd scribbled this little saying on the front cover.
> *'Evil be to him who thinks evil.'*[40]

It's one of the things he used to say.

On the back, random words and phrases had been jotted down. 'Black Prince', 'Richard II', 'Rodney Ayton, Steward' and 'Christopher Fleet, Armourer'. It's curious.

---

[40] A loose translation of "Honi Soit Qui Mal Pense" - Motto of the Order of the Garter

155

This was dad's chair by the fire in the drawing room at home.

He read the Telegraph and drank tea in this chair.

When I was little it took us on adventures. I'd climb on dad's knee and the chair became a car, or a pony and trap, or a boat on the estuary.

The chair's arms are wide with flat tops. My journal is on one arm, a bowl of peanuts on the other.

The bowl is a souvenir from my holiday in La Reole. It's identical to the ones in the cafe there.

I use it for my peanuts.

I love their salty crunch.

I the like the feel more than the taste.

I pick out the half nuts first, saving the whole ones until the end.

I eat the whole ones in order from the smallest to the largest.

It seems silly to write in such detail. I guess keeping this journal has made me reflect on detail. I've learned they're often more important than bigger things.

I still feel fragile.

Concentrating on my peanuts, helps me find focus.

I wonder if real happiness is in these little things.

I'm learning to give more time to such things.

Take that meal Tess gave me: flaked truffle on scrambled eggs.

So simple.

Such pleasure.

She's perfect.

I can't wait to see her tomorrow. It'll be a treat. She can't be far off the age of that girl Rachel from the Aperitivo yesterday.

I saw scars when Rachel wore that pretty dress on the train. So many cuts. I wonder if she cut herself just to feel? I think some do that.

I'm going to take time to sip my beer and look out over the garden.

Music is playing.

I'm listening to Nina Simone.

I'm Feeling Good.

What's not to like?

Sublime.

Then, You Gotta Serve Somebody.

I know Bob Dylan wrote it.

Those words, 'You gotta serve somebody'[41] strike a chord and direct my attention back to the guide book.

Dad wrote:
> *'Evil be to him who thinks evil.'*[42]

He hated double-standards and people doing down others and or not keeping their word.

Dad could be a pain in the arse, but I loved him.

I'm down to the last few nuts and scraping up the salt and those nobbly little square bits in the bottom of the bowl.

In fact my pen's a bit slippy in my hand from the oiliness of the peanuts as I write this and I've made I one or two grease marks on the pages.

I've enjoyed just letting my mind wander tonight, especially after my meltdown yesterday.

I'd better get off to bed. It's a big day tomorrow.

---

[41] B Dylan B, Special Rider Music (1979)

[42] A loose translation of, "Honi Soit Qui Mal Pense" - Motto of the Order of the Garter

157

Day 39

I'm in Aperitivo waiting for Tess at the very table I began writing my journal. She's meeting me for coffee.

It took three hours at Scarab this morning. I came straight here. I thought I'd be late. Anyway I'm here now and I've done it at last, with no regrets. That said, at this precise moment I have an ache in my shoulder and a weird feeling from clingfilm wrapped round it.

I can see Tess through the cafe window. She's listening to the busker under the arch of the Buttercross. The two of them are framed there. They look for all the world, a Pre-Raphaelite tableau. Tess with her flowing hair and the busker, her minstrel muse.

It's just my impression.

My imagination has run beyond reality.

I suppose that's the point of imagination.

The scene has no more meaning than a young woman listening to a young man playing and singing.

My private reality is that Tess is my muse; the stuff my dreams are made of.

Why shouldn't that be so?

She's broken the tableau and walked out of its frame in the Buttercross arch. She's coming over to meet me now.

INTERLUDE WHILST I HAVE COFFEE AND CAKE WITH TESS

Tess has gone now. I'm back to writing my journal. I'll pick up where I left off.

I described Tess as my muse. That's the right word. She has the divine about her. I can't explain it. I don't want to try. It's enough for her just to be.

She came through the cafe door, arms open to hug me. It was the same when she left. I loved that. I don't know what the best adjective is to describe her. There's just a lightness to her, a gentleness.

She sat across the table from me, a delicate frame, with porcelain complexion and a mass of tumbling hair scrunched into a loose ash-blond ponytail. The early afternoon sun poured over her through the cafe window. She moved round and sat beside me.

I noticed she wore a black teardrop pearl nestled in her salt cellar[43].

It's a strange name, 'salt cellar'. Mum would have called it that.

We had such a lovely time over coffee and lemon drizzle cake. We share something very special. I still don't know if it's proper.

It turns out she knows the busker through an LGBTQ+ group and Pride in York. Apparently, his name is Adam.

I don't understand all this LGBTQ+ business. I asked Tess about it and now I'm even more confused. She says there are eight or nine more letters. How many options do they need!

Evidently she sees herself as 'Q'. I gather it stands for 'Questioning' and 'Queer'.

She didn't elaborate.

I didn't ask.

I have the impression they're quite different.

I'm not sure.

I'm not sure why can't they decide on 'Q' for either Queer or Questioning.

When I was young Queer covered all of the option, other than 'normal'. It was easier then; straight and queer.

I've caught myself thinking about what mum used to say if someone did something she didn't expect: 'that's a bit queer', followed by, 'it's not normal'.

Tess tried to explain. She says she's 'non-binary'. There's another term to add to the list: 'non-binary'.

What she said about 'non-binary' was so interesting.

The penny dropped when she described wanting look beyond gender and sexuality and wanting to see the 'soul', the essence of a person at the core of who they are. She used a metaphor that brought it all to life for me. She described people as a 'constellations of identities'. I like that!

---

[43] The term 'salt cellar' is a slightly poetic and archaic term for the jugular notch, the point where the two collar bones meet at the base of the neck.

I can see it in myself: at work, here in Aperitivo, in the Ring O' Bells, a 'constellation of identities', the same person in all these different places, but seen in slightly different ways.

I like this idea of stripping away the layers and seeing the person. It doesn't feel that different to wanting people to know the 'me' inside, the person I really am rather than the 'I', another person sees.

Tess reckons society is controlled by people like me: white, middle-class, straight, male. It was difficult to hear. She says people like me hold all the power and make all the real decisions.

I'm thinking about that girl we interviewed, Clementine Nnadi. There were two camps, those who didn't want to interview her because of her African name and those who thought she'd tick the diversity box. It turns out she's brilliant. I'm not sure we appointed her because she's brilliant.

Back to Adam the busker. Tess says he, 'Sings other people's songs, never his own'. It's funny, I remember Adam sitting with the whey-faced lad at the next table a few weeks ago. He seemed passionate enough to me.

I don't think Tess's thoughts are anyone else's but her own.

She's not completely feral. She's from someone and somewhere. Pearl is her someone and Cambridge her somewhere, growing up in that house on Beaver road. - It's said Beaver and spelled Belvior. I've walked down there on my way to the river and boathouses. If only I'd known Pearl lived there.

Belvoir reminds me of Belvoir Castle on the way to Cambridge. Mum's people were from near there, from Oakham. We visited. The castle was ripped apart in the civil war, just like Elsternwick. More fanatics, leaving scars.

I'm going off my own point.

Tess gave me such a lot to think about. I've never had such conversation over lemon drizzle cake and coffee. I want to think she's 'tilting at windmills' as the saying goes. I don't want to admit she has a point.

I can see she is finding her own way, asking her own questions.

Isn't that what I've been doing in my journal?

I'd better get home. My shoulder is really itchy now. I want to get some air to it.

Day 40

I'm at the kitchen table, beginning to write the last entry in my journal. As I think about what to write, I'm looking through the open kitchen doorway and into the hall. I can see the painting of the girl across the river hanging there. It was the first thing I commented on at the start of this journal. The girl's image is so subtle, an impression in the brush strokes.

I've poured myself a huge glass of merlot and set music to play random songs. I can't believe the irony in the first one:
> 'Rolling home to you.'[44]
I've been with Pearl and Tom tonight!

It's been an amazing evening.

Pearl and I ended our evening at the bench in Elsternwick marketplace. I offered to take her home, but she wasn't having it. She said she had a taxi booked, which was true.

Actually, it felt right to end the evening at the bench. It's where it all began again with Pearl last year.

Before getting into her taxi, she took the squashy envelope I have here out of her bag and gave it to me. My name is on the front in faded ink. It looks years old. I'm tempted to open it will leave it here on the kitchen table until the morning.

I've put a rose petal next to the envelope. I picked the petal up in the church when Pearl and I wandered in this evening. I sneaked it from a display.

I met Pearl in the churchyard tonight. She in her, 'dressed as a hooker' mode.

It's ironic, I met someone looking like a hooker in a churchyard.

I gave her back the leopard print scarf as soon as we met. I wanted to drape it round her neck but it didn't feel right. I just handed it to her instead. She put it round her own neck without a word. That was that, the sum of our greeting.

We walked closely through the churchyard, hands almost touching and without a word. The silence felt right. Actually the word, 'silence' isn't right. 'Quiet' is the right word. Silence is cold and empty.

---

[44] N Young, Label Reprise (1972)

We stepped through the arch into Hag's Wynd and sat on the mounting block, our backs against the ruins of the town walls. It's where we'd sit when we were young.

Yellow and orange crocus peppered the lawn around us.

We sat in our quiet, hands settled on the mounting block.

Pearl touched my little finger with hers, linking it over mine then pulling away.

It was just a moment. The gentlest of nothing.

I focused on the quiet.

Pearl broke it.

She told me how they'd drag women past the mounting block tied to a 'cucking stool'. Then they'd drag then down the steep bank across the path from us so they could hurl the women into the Woscen Pool for 'trial by water', to see if they were witches. Apparently, if they sank and drowned, they were deemed 'innocent' and 'guilty' if they floated. The guilty were hurled over the Hag's Force and left for dead, flesh eaten by rats and foxes.

I'd always thought It was 'ducking stool'. She said 'cucking'.

I suppose that's where they get cuckold from, as in Shagging Sheila's husband, the 'cuckold'. I wonder what they'd have done to Shagging Sheila?

I wonder what they'd have done to Pearl, dressed like a hooker?

I'm not sure what I think?

Our quiet had been broken by the story.

There were squabbling young ravens above us in the treetops. I watched them flapping and *cawing* in the silhouette tree tops, mottling lines against the fading light of the evening's grey sky.

On the mounting block, there was only us. It felt like we'd never been away.

Distractions didn't matter.

I didn't mind her stories.

She told me about the She Wolf, forced to marry Edward II and no more than a child.

She told me about the She Wolf's loves and passions and invasion from France to overthrow the king. I've read The She Wolf.[45] It's good.

Quiet returned.

I fumbled for the little green box from Cavendish's and tried to be subtle.

I can be cack-handed.

I think 'cack' means shit. It's 'shit-handed', clumsy, left-handed. It's true, I felt clumsy. I passed the box from my left hand jacket pocket and into my right hand. I put it on the mounting block between us.

She picked it up, without a word and hardly a gesture. She fingered it, turning it slowly and gently. She set it on her lap against the chrome zipper of her black leather mini-skirt. She held it there.

I tried not to look.

Quiet returned.

The young ravens squabbled in their roost.

Pearl went on with her stories. I knew the next one. It was about Edward III and letters patent, allowing the walls and a tower house for the Steward as a reward for sending archers to Crecy.

Quiet returned.

The young ravens were silent.

There was nothing but us.

She broke the quiet, saying we needed to get moving.

We went through the arch and into the churchyard. Almost passing the church, she insisted we go in.

There were two pools of light in the church's gloom. One was from a spotlight shining on an empty table; the other from an angle poise lamp shining on a single rose, its petals torn and scattered around. The petal I have here is one I took for myself. I don't know why I took it. I picked up a service sheet too. I read these words:

---

[45] M Droun, She Wolf, Harper Colins (1955)

How many of us have known what it is to be crushed, torn and ravaged.
How many of us 'remember we are dust'.
You are this rose.   Beautiful, yet torn.
You are this rose.   Beautiful, once whole.
You are this rose.   Beauty now faded?

I sat in the church's quiet.

I thought about beauty no-one sees.

Pearl sat beside me.

Taking my hand she stood and led the way out of the gloom of the church, through the lychgate and over the marketplace to the Queens.

I've no idea why she took my hand.

She has the hand of a child.

I tried to be gentle, barely holding.

She pulled away at the Queen's and led the way to the Snug.

The Snug is called a 'private dining room' now but still smells of stale beer. It was a place for old men years ago. They taught us cribbage in the Snug saying 'Play the player, not the hand'.

Tom was there when we arrived. He held out his hands to take mine. His grip was weak. His shake was wringing with enthusiasm.

I noticed his knuckles, red and flaking with psoriasis.

Frank, at the office has psoriasis. I know it can be a dreadful condition but Frank picks his scalp and flicks flakes of dry skin around. Disgusting!

Tom and I didn't hug.

Tom's smile was as I remembered. A boy's smile, only empty.

He greeted Pearl with a hug. She did that thing she does, tucking her head against his chest, avoiding a glancing kiss.

We sat as we used to.

I had my back to the curved wall, with its massive stone block-work. Pearl sat next to me, as she always did. Tom was across the table from us, as he always was.

At first, we didn't say much. We talked facts and events.

We spoke of the paths we'd followed in life, at least that was so for Tom and me.

Pearl was quiet.

When Tom told his story, he used the repeating phrase, 'leaning into webs'[46] like a motif, a pattern.

He spoke of being tangled up by people who hung him out to dry.

He called one 'the bitch' and spoke of the 'bitch's web'.

I remember Kevin telling me about this 'bitch' and how their father said she should be unremembered.

'Unremembered.' I suppose that's being scrubbed out: annihilated. That must be hell, annihilation: true death, far beyond alone.

I flushed with tears at Tom's story, looked straight ahead. I tried to hide the tears.

Pearl knew. Somehow she knew. She gently squeezed my thigh under the table.

I've no idea how she knew.

I loved Tom's happy ending.

It seems the tangled web was cut by Janet Field, she of the budding tits and frizzy hair.

Tom said she'd just had an impulse to call him and that she didn't know why. She simply followed her impulse.

It turns out, she called at the exact moment Tom had slung a noose over a beam in his office, about to end it all.

Tom said he'd been so shocked by the call, he told Janet what he was doing and she shouted down the phone bringing him to his senses.

---

[46] Job 8.14

167

What a good job she called him, followed her instincts and took the trouble. She changed the course of events.

Tom said, Janet's call brought him to his senses.

He said it was as if the scales fell way from his eyes and he saw the truth; that he'd been played by those he's thought he could trust. The web of deceit had become a knot around him. Janet sliced through it in an instant.

Tom said he felt like a fly caught in a spider's web and realised a spider waits for its tangled victim to struggle. So he chose keep very still, to take control.

As I sit here and write about what Tom said, I'm struck how there was strength in his voice as he said, 'She's unremembered.' 'She's dead.' 'The bitch doesn't matter'.

I can see what Tom's father meant, true death is to be unremembered. That is annihilation.

Anyway, important though that may be, Pearl reached across, took my hand and pulled it to her. I felt the chrome zipper of her black leather mini-skirt against the back of my hand. She held it there.

I couldn't look. I didn't need to. It was enough to feel her soft, childlike hand pressed into mine as I listened to Tom.

In that moment and in that gesture, Pearl held me, really held me.

What are these bonds between people that make a gesture's touch feel like an embrace leading one to rescue the other?

Tonight in the Snug and siting here at my kitchen table, I recognise it was in that place and with those friends I was hewn, formed and fashioned for life. I admit, it's humbling to recognise that with those friends and that place, I belong.

I ought to get to bed or I'll be siting in my kitchen all night. Before I do, I want to have a look at the envelope Pearl gave me. There are some words written along one edge in that faded handwriting. I can just make them out:
   '......We are linked as children in a circle dancing'[47].
What a strange thing to write? Nevertheless I see the truth in them. I cannot deny it.

Glancing into the hall to the painting, it's as if the impression of the girl across the river has disappeared. How odd? I wonder how that is so?

---

[47] W.H. Auden, Miranda's Song, (The Sea and the Mirror, II), (1943)